Behind the
of Historic Marietta

Behind the Doors of Historic Marietta

Late 1890's Marietta
*Courtesy of Washington County Public Library,
Local History and Genealogy*

Jann Kuehn Adams

Copyright © 2011 by Jann Kuehn Adams
All rights reserved
2nd printing 2014

Published by Jann Kuehn Adams
Marietta, OH
contact: jannkadams@gmail.com

No part of this publication may be reproduced, stored in, or introduced into a retrieval system, or transmitted in any form or by any means (electronic, mechanical, photocopying, recording or otherwise) without prior written permission of both the copyright owner and the publisher of this book.

Design and Layout
Cernus Printing Consultants, Ink (CPC, Ink)
Dona J. Cernus
Marietta, Ohio

Cover: Photos by Jann Kuehn Adams
Historical Site Pages: Photos by Jann Kuehn Adams

ISBN 978-1-4507-5909-0

Printed in the United States
February 2011

Acknowledgment

A very special thank you to The Marietta Chapter of The American Association of University Women who published the first edition (1986) and the second edition (1996) of *A Window To Marietta*. Unfortunately, the group closed the local chapter in 2009, bringing to an end the publication of *A Window To Marietta*. The closing of that publication inspired me to research the history of Marietta through the doors of our historical buildings and with our existing monuments. My hope with the publication of *Behind the Doors of Historic Marietta*, visitors and local citizens, will once again have access to Marietta's hidden history.

I would also like to thank the following people for assisting me with this project: Dona Cernus, Deborah Kiefer, Toni Leland, Harley Noland, Linda Showalter, and Cathy Schafer.

Preface

Welcome to historic Marietta. If you are like many visitors to our city, you find yourself standing at the fountain on the levee overlooking the Ohio River and thinking, "What is the story of Marietta?" Usually people know that it was the first settlement of the Northwest Territory, but then query, "What was this territory and why was it significant?"

Marietta's old buildings hold a hidden heritage, a history long forgotten by time, new businesses, and new residents. Local museums offer a history teeming with authentic and vintage items allowing visitors to truly imagine living in the times of early Marietta. However, it is the ambiance of the brick streets, the Victorian shops and homes, the waterfront, and the gentle feeling of peacefulness that draw people into a feeling of contentment in quaint Marietta. It is the look and feel of Marietta that engage the visitor with the sense of the past.

Like historical documents and old newspapers that are securely hidden away, our old buildings can tell the story of Marietta. They are standing proof of the people, businesses, political savvy, and determination of the early pioneers and those who immigrated here in the mid-to late nineteenth century to build a city. The purpose of this book is to explore the structures of the 1800's and early 1900's as a way to unfold "history on location." By observing the places of yesterday, the book will draw out the history held by these walls built of brick, board, and stone. This is not a comprehensive text, but a walk in the shoes of some of the people who built the city of Marietta.

HOW TO USE THIS BOOK

The book is intended as a reference book in which each page stands alone. You may use this guide while walking or driving around the streets of Marietta. The map in the back of the book shows places of interest numbered to match the page on which you find the history. The pages are arranged in an order to facilitate driving to each of the sites. Enjoy your visit.

Contents

Introduction 13
Historic Harmar District, **Harmar Village**............................... 14
Harmar Railroad Bridge.. 15
David Putnam House 16
Douglas Pattin House.. 17
James Whitney House... 18
Levi Barber House 19
Fort Harmar Marker 20
Dr. Seth Hart House 21
Henry Fearing House 22
Benjamin Ives Gilman 23
Children's Toy & Doll Museum... 24
Old Harmar Congregational Church 25
Anchorage-Putnam Villa... 26
The Mill 27

Historic Downtown Marietta 28
Bicentennial Plaza 29
Picketed Point Marker... 30
The Gay Nineties in Marietta.. 31
Lafayette Hotel... 35
Schafer building 36
Flood Markers 37
The Register Building 38
D. B. Anderson building 39
Monument to the 48 Pioneers 40
Lock Keeper's House 41
Old Post Office... 42
Bank of Marietta 43
First Congregational Church... 44
Return Jonathan Meigs, Jr. House... 45
The Monument To Start Westward 46
Buckley House 47
Shipman House 48
Holden House... 49
Ohio River Museum 50
Marietta Brewing Company.. 51
Campus Martius Museum 52

Sacra Via Park	57
B. E. Stoehr House	58
Washington County Public Library	59
Larchmont	60
St. Luke's Episcopal Church	61
Washington County Court House	62
New Riley Block	63
Tiber Way	64
Levee House Café	65
The Flatiron District	66
Shipbuilding Monument	69
Old St. Mary's Catholic School	70
Unitarian Universalist Church	71
Bosworth-Biszantz House	72
Old Third Street School Annex	73
Crown of Life Evangelical Lutheran Church	74
Dawes House	75
Basilica of St. Mary of the Assumption	76
Shipman-Mills House	77
The Castle	78
St. Luke's Lutheran Church	79
Betsey Mills Club	80
Macmillen House	81
Marietta College Campus	82
Mills Home	83
Erwin Hall	84
Andrews Hall	85
Flanders House	86
George White House	87
House of Seven Porches	88
St. Paul's Evangelical Church	89
Mound Cemetery	90
Josiah D. Cotton House	91
Clark-Van Metre House	92
Thomas Cisler House	93
Old Childrens Home	94
Afterward	95
Glossary of Architectural Terms	97
Selective Bibliography	99
About the Author	101
Map	inside back cover

Introduction

Part of the American bounty at the conclusion of the Revolutionary War was the acquisition of the Northwest Territory by the United States. Today, the present-day states of Ohio, Indiana, Illinois, Michigan, Wisconsin, and part of Minnesota make up that territory. Marietta, located at the confluence of the Ohio and Muskingum Rivers, was the first permanent settlement in this new frontier. After an overland route and a trip down the Ohio River with flatboats, the first pioneers were greeted on April 7, 1788 by the soldiers of Fort Harmar, which had been established earlier to protect the territorial land and the native peoples who lived here.

Marietta, named in honor of Queen Marie Antoinette of France for supporting the War of Independence, was designed to be a city demonstrating law, order, education, and religion in the frontier. The Ohio Company of Associates, led by Rufus Putnam, wanted the town to reflect their New England roots. Many of the original forty-eight pioneers were officers in the Revolutionary War who had invested in over a million acres of land. Early businesses and cabins were established along the confluence of the Ohio and Muskingum Rivers at Picketed Point. Fearing attack from Indians who had grown restless with the increasing encroachment of white settlers, Campus Martius, a fortification along the Muskingum River, was built and used for several years until the Indian Wars ended.

Marietta business thrived along the Ohio River and the population grew. This small town welcomed settlers and supported those traveling on down river to other communities by supplying them with goods. The port of Marietta was a bustling place: boats arrived and departed daily, engaged in trade, brought mail and new settlers. Between 1890 and 1910, Marietta businesses flourished and the population doubled, mostly due to a huge oil boom in Washington County. The Victorian Era architecture has left its mark on the homes and business buildings in downtown Marietta and Harmar.

Harmar Village
West side of Muskingum River in vicinity of Maple Street

With the opening of Fort Harmar in 1785, the Harmar district held the earliest United States military occupation in the Northwest Territory. When the pioneers came in 1788, they claimed the east side of the Muskingum River for settlement. In 1801, Marietta was incorporated to include the Harmar district located on the west side of the river. Many prominent people built their homes in Harmar, particularly on Fort Street where the ground was higher than on Front Street. Harmar held the first Bank of Marietta, premiered tremendous shipbuilding ventures, and provided basic businesses for the area. It was also the site of the first official cemetery for Marietta.

With discontent in Harmar over various issues unknown today, the citizens of the west side decided to break away from Marietta and operate as a separate village in 1837. A government was formed with James Whitney, shipbuilder, serving as the first mayor. Harmar's post office can still be seen as a historic site on Gilman Avenue. On May 15, 1890, Harmar voted to rejoin Marietta.

Harmar prospered in the nineteenth century with business ventures on the waterfront and in the village. In the early 1800's, shipbuilding was at a peak with the Gilman and Whitney boatyards until the Embargo Act brought it to a halt. By 1860, big businesses found success in Harmar. The Marietta Bucket Factory, operated by John Newton, was a leading business. A.T. Nye & Son owned the Marietta Foundry that equipped many homes and businesses with stoves. The well-known Putnam brothers ran a dry goods store and the Eagle Wooden Ware Works and the Barbers had a grocery and dry goods store. The Exchange Hotel, later to house the Steven's Organ and Piano Company, prospered on Gilman Avenue.

Between 1890 and 1910, downtown Harmar took advantage of the good economy of the Gay Nineties. In the second half of the century, the Knox boatyards were well-known for building steam-powered sternwheelers for transportation of goods and people. Pattin Brothers, George Strecker & Company, and the Marietta Manufacturing Company were all leaders in boiler making, some with a specialty in steamboat machinery. There were milliners, dressmakers, druggists, furniture dealers, physicians, and a flour mill. Buchanon's Drug Store, Detzel's Novelty Shop, Gilcher's Groceries, Neader's Barbershop, Storck's Bakery, and Tornes's Boots conducted business on Maple Street. The area boasted of the American House, a hotel, and the Detzel Sample Room that also had a pool and billiard room. The 1891 Board of Trade said this of Detzel's business: "trade of the house is confined to the better class of people and the place is the resort par excellence of the gentle man of Marietta." Even though Harmar had rejoined Marietta in 1890, it continued to be a thriving village of its own.

Today, you can visit shops and eateries located in the original business district. Homes of notable Marietta people from times past are still in use by residents, businesses, and museums.

Harmar Railroad Bridge
Crosses the Muskingum River linking Harmar Village and downtown Marietta

In 1987, the Historic Harmar Village Bridge Company completed a pedestrian walkway across the old railroad bridge on the Muskingum River. Visitors and local residents enjoy the scenic view while walking or biking across the historic bridge that connects Harmar Village and downtown Marietta.

The Harmar Railroad Bridge has a history of starts and stops. Finances and floods made it difficult to establish a connection across the river. The Marietta and Cincinnati Railroad began to build a bridge to Marietta from the west side of the Muskingum River in the 1850's, but the company went bankrupt before the bridge was completed. In 1857, it opened as a two-lane covered bridge for pedestrians and horse-drawn vehicles. The five westernmost piers of the present bridge are the original piers of 1856/1857.

Marietta and Cincinnati Railroad made another attempt to build a stronger bridge in 1873, but the flood of 1884 eventually destroyed the structure. It was rebuilt with the second pier on the east side holding the turntable of the draw span that was erected in 1895. This span would be turned by hand to allow the passage of tall boats. This structure was used until the great flood of 1913 destroyed it again. In 1922, the first pier on the east side was built and traffic was restored. In general, the bridge was used for railroad traffic from 1873-1962.

David Putnam House
519 Fort Street

Local lore tells us that men from Fort Harmar began work on this house in 1792. It was completed in 1805 for David Putnam, the son of Colonel Israel Putnam of Belpre and a distant cousin of Rufus Putnam, leader of the first pioneers to Marietta. Stone for the walls was quarried on Harmar Hill. This building housed the first bank of the Northwest Territory and Ohio, chartered in 1808. Rufus Putnam was the bank's first president. David Putnam was a director and the cashier. The Putnam family residence was located above the bank which occupied the first floor.

David Putnam held company with the founding members of Marietta who were ardent in their desires to create civility in the town bordering the frontier. Putnam, a Yale University graduate, was the director of the co-educational Muskingum Academy which opened in 1800. During the Temperance Movement, he headed the Society for the Promotion of Good Morals and urged the Ohio governor to penalize public intoxication. His sons, David, Jr. and Douglas, were both well-known and respected businessmen. David, Jr. was an ardent abolitionist and an active conductor of local Underground Railroad activities.

Seven generations of the Putnam family owned and lived in this Federal Period house. In the 1920's, Benjamin Barnes Putnam extensively renovated and restored it. In the 1930's, the house was temporarily "The Marietta Home of Today" featuring the latest electrical equipment for modern living. The original bank vault was removed from the basement during that time. The house was a private residence until the late 1980's before becoming an office building.

Douglas Pattin House
521 Fort Street

When coming across the Putnam Street Bridge into Harmar, visitors are drawn to the beautiful stone house on the left. The grand house at the end of north Fort Street is a showcase in the use of stone. Notice the small hearts, which celebrate the Hart connection of the original owner, carved in the stone columns at the entry. Quarried locally, the stone has been rusticated, or cut in facets, instead of straight across as the cut stone of the Putnam house next door. Several stone masons' signature marks are visible on the exterior. Be sure to look at the unique chimneys that add an interesting effect to the roofline. Large homes of this period, like this one, had grand ballrooms on the third floor for entertainment.

The oil and natural gas boom of the late 1800's brought business opportunity and wealth to many families in Marietta. Douglas P. and Mary Hart Pattin were pleased to finish this home in 1899. Douglas and his brother, Winfield, were partners in Pattin Brothers & Company, a successful general machine business that specialized in steam pumps, oil well supplies, and apparatuses. In 1899, a new plant was built on Second Street as an addition to the original plant in Harmar. While investigating a gas leak at his Second Street business, Douglas P. Pattin was killed in an explosion in 1901. Newspaper headlines gave the details of the disaster and mourned the loss of this well-known businessman.

The house served as a residence for several families until 1988. The advertising firm of Offenberger and White adapted the rooms as office space while retaining the historical character. For their efforts they earned a Preservation Merit Award by the Ohio Historical Society in 1990.

James Whitney House
415 Fort Street

Most local people probably do not know the name, James Whitney, an "unsung" influence in the early ship business. James Whitney, a master ship builder, worked for Benjamin Ives Gilman boat yard, known for producing ocean-going vessels. In 1800, the *St. Clair,* built in Marietta and captained by Abraham Whipple, reached Havana, Cuba. This set off an economic boom in shipbuilding and the transport of local goods overseas. Several merchants commissioned James Whitney to build boats ready for international waters. In 1802, the building of ocean-going ships was so successful that the federal government opened a local office to register ships. James Whitney was named surveyor of the port of Marietta. Between 1802 and 1808, Whitney built nine ships, brigs, and schooners. Ships were built until 1808 when the U.S. Embargo Act, forbidding ships from leaving ports to go to parts of Europe, ruined the business. Mr. Whitney opened a store and later owned a steam sawmill. In 1837, he became the first mayor of Harmar (when it was a village separate from Marietta). Following the death of James Whitney in 1852, a number of people have resided in the house.

This Neo Georgian style two-story frame house overlooks the confluence of the Ohio and Muskingum Rivers, a perfect setting for a shipbuilder. The rear wing was built about 1833 and the front part of house was completed in 1847. At one time, the house had a Victorian front porch, but it was removed. The fluted Doric pilasters and a transom remain. The stairs in the entry are unusual in design: they appear to be similar to stairs leading to the pilothouse of riverboats.

Levi Barber House
407 Fort Street

The setting of the Levi Barber house provides an incredible view of the confluence of the Ohio and Muskingum Rivers. In the early 1800's, lots on Fort Street were popular building sites because the land set at a higher elevation than much of downtown Marietta. Joseph Barker, a well-known builder of the day, constructed the house in 1829. Keeping with the popular Federal style architecture, it is symmetrical in design, having a central door with fan and sidelights of colored glass. The same arrangement is found in a second floor window over the door. Brick for the house was fired in a kiln located on Gilman Avenue in the vicinity of what is now the Marietta College Boathouse.

Colonel Levi Barber, the first owner, came to Ohio from New England in 1799 as a surveyor for the federal government. Because of his job, he was given the land free of charge. During his lifetime in Marietta, Barber became involved in politics at the county and federal levels of government. He was elected to the Ohio House of Representatives in 1806, clerk of the circuit courts of Common Pleas and the court in Washington County from 1809-1817, aide to Governor Meigs in the War of 1812, and served in the U.S. Congress from 1816-1822. Colonel Barber was also the fourth president of the Bank of Marietta, the first bank chartered in Ohio. In his later years, he was appointed Trustee of Ohio University in Athens, Ohio and held the position until his death in 1833.

The Barber House is one of the few homes in the Marietta area that has been occupied by the same family for generations. In a 2010 remodeling project, the original, hand-dug well was found in perfect condition, formed with curved cut stone block. Sealed with a glass top and highlighted with an inside light, it has become part of the floor in the new kitchen.

Fort Harmar Marker
Intersection of Fort Street and Market Street

It is believed that Fort Harmar was located near the present-day site of Harmar Elementary School. Following the American Revolution, the Northwest Territory was ceded to the Americans by the British and this opened up the lands north and west of the Ohio River for settlement. If unwatched, it was feared Indian treaties would be violated and policies of the Continental Congress would not be honored. Colonel Josiah Harmar ordered Captain John Doughty to build a post at the mouth of the Muskingum River to protect Indian lands and to dispel settlers from "squatting" on the land. Fort Harmar was one of the first forts in the Northwest Territory, land controlled by the newly independent United States.

Fort Harmar, named for the commanding officer Colonel Josiah Harmar, was built in the shape of a pentagon with an area of less than one acre. Large timbers were placed horizontally 12 feet wide, 15 feet high, and 120 feet long to form the walls of defense. A square tower was built to afford a view of the surrounding area. Soldiers cultivated gardens to provide ample vegetables, and planted fruit trees. In the center of the fort was a well for water, in case of an attack. (Interestingly, because the rivers have become wider and deeper, it is believed the original fort would have been located in the Ohio River.)

On April 7, 1788, Marietta's first pioneers accidentally arrived at Fort Harmar when they overshot the mouth of the Muskingum River because of fog and overhanging trees. With the assistance of the soldiers, they were redirected to the eastern shore.

Dr. Seth Hart House
115 Gilman Avenue

Though this humble 1810 dwelling is aged, we are still fortunate to have it standing as an example of a typical early Federal style house. The two-story structure is covered with stucco and painted in a buff color to model stone. The house has survived all of the recorded major floods in the area. It was built in an elevated position to protect it from high water. The small symmetrically-placed windows, the narrow transom over the central door, and plain front steps are typical of the period.

Dr. Seth Hart, a well-known doctor of the mid 1800's, served the medical needs of the community with house calls and homemade medicine. He raised a family in this home and had his office in a building next door. Hart, born in Connecticut, received a liberal education in the State of New York. There he taught school, studied medicine, and clerked in a drug store until 1824 when he came to New Philadelphia, Ohio, where he once again taught school. The same year, he received a diploma which qualified him for medical practice. Dr. Hart lived briefly in Washington County's Watertown until 1836 when he came to Harmar. Dr. Hart prepared all of his own medicine and occasionally returned to New York to attend lectures on medicine. In 1857, Hart and his son, Samuel, opened up an office on Front Street. Concerned about being able to continue to serve the residents of Harmar, they announced that arrangements would be made with the Muskingum Ferry. The people of Harmar could cross the river and call on the office any hour of the day or night. The dispensary included Dr. Hart's homemade Croup Syrup, Cough Syrup, and the Napoleon Cure for Kidney Disease. In 1865, Dr. Hart went to Tennessee to help his son at an Army hospital at the close of the Civil War. He was commissioned a surgeon of the Fifth Tennessee Cavalry. His son, Samuel, continued the medical practice in Marietta.

Henry Fearing House
131 Gilman Avenue

The Fearing family, early settlers to Marietta, made their mark by their service to the community. Paul Fearing, a Harvard law graduate, came to Marietta in May of 1788 and practiced law at Fort Harmar. He was the first lawyer in the Northwest Territory. His son, Henry, built this two-story brick house on the corner of Market Street and Gilman Avenue in 1847. Locally, Fearing was a businessman who developed property and had various investments, including part interest in a steamboat. He helped to raise money to support the construction of the Woman's Home built in 1885 in Marietta. Fearing, active in the Whig party, was also an advocate for the Temperance Movement. In education efforts, he was a trustee of the Harmar Academy. His daughter, Carolyn, was the mother-in-law of Unites States Vice President Charles G. Dawes of Marietta. Benjamin Dana Fearing, a son, was one of the five Civil War generals from Washington County. Henry Fearing lived in this house until his death in 1894.

The house of the Federal Period and of Neo Georgian style is a basic rectangular structure of brick set on a cut sandstone foundation. The shallow-pitched hipped roof and windows arranged symmetrically around a center doorway are typical for the period. In 1870, an addition was attached on the south side.

In 1974, the Washington County Historical Society purchased the house. After a long renovation, it was dedicated as a museum in 1983. The museum, containing many artifacts, depicts the lifestyle of Marietta's middle class during the Victorian Era.

Benjamin Ives Gilman
Intersection of Gilman Avenue and Market Street

Gilman Avenue was named for Benjamin Ives Gilman who built his house in the early 1800's at the intersection of the present-day streets of Gilman and Market Streets. Part of the original structure still stands, but a huge, square front addition was attached in the 1840's. The rear section is likely to be the oldest house in Harmar. The fan window on the gable behind the front roof gives a hint of the original back house. The Gilman family lived in the house until 1813 when they moved to Philadelphia. The house passed out of the Gilman family possession in 1833, so the original family never saw the 1840 addition to the front.

Benjamin Ives Gilman, a well-known shipbuilder, probably built his house at this intersection when his shipbuilding business flourished in the early 1800's. As a young man, he came to Harmar with his parents and lived in the fort during the Indian Wars of the 1790's. He had a store at the fort from 1792 until 1812. B. I. Gilman was a shipwright, house builder, and merchant who was also a shareholder and agent for the Ohio Company. Gilman was a wealthy, influential Federalist who owned over 22,000 acres of land as well as a shipyard along the Muskingum River. As a member of the first Ohio Constitutional Convention from Washington County, he voted to keep Ohio a free state. In the early 1800's, Marietta was a center for shipbuilding, and Gilman held company with at least four other major shipbuilders and owners. Due to the number of ocean-going ships built here, Gilman was part of a group who gained permission from the U.S. government to allow Marietta to be a port to register boats. Gilman shipyard was busy between 1803-1814. The Embargo Act of 1807 delivered a severe blow to the international ship industry.

Children's Toy & Doll Museum
206 Gilman Avenue

The Children's Toy & Doll Museum has the honor to be housed in one of Harmar's Victorian Era homes. Built in 1889, the house reflects the Queen Anne/Eastlake style of architecture with the steep roofs, an irregular shape, and the two-sided porch. The house has several bay windows, particularly notable are first and second story bays on the side of the house. When it was purchased in 1996 by the museum, the home was in need of extensive repairs and renovation. The museum contains outstanding collections of antique dolls, vintage toys, and miniatures. Themed rooms include fairy tale dollhouses, circus memorabilia, and antique children's toys.

George S. Strecker, a Harmar boilermaker from Germany, built this house on Gilman not far from his business. His wife, Johanna, was the architect. Strecker was a well-known and respected businessman in Marietta. His main business interest was the George Strecker & Company established in 1867, and it manufactured oil stills, tanks, marine boilers, and smoke stacks. From 1882 to 1887, Rodrick Brothers and Strecker were owners of the sternwheeler, *Olivette*. Built at the Knox boat yard in Harmar, the low water packet ran trades on the Muskingum River up to Zanesville. Strecker was successful enough to broaden his business interest by building a flour mill in 1884 on Lancaster Street.

Old Harmar Congregational Church
301 Franklin Street

Built in 1847, this structure is the oldest church building still in use in Marietta. The main church building is of Greek Revival style with the pediment roof and pilasters located on the exterior walls. An added feature is the octagonal cupola for use as a bell tower. The building addition on the right is of Gothic Revival style architecture, which gives the church a softer look with the pointed windows.

Part of the intent of the pioneers who founded Marietta was to assure that civility reigned in the Northwest Territory. Church participation was important. Before the first bridge was built across the Muskingum River, the only way for the people of Harmar to attend church was to pay for a ferry on Sunday mornings to cross the river to attend services held at the Front Street Congregational Church. In 1840, Reverend Joel Harvey Lindsey (Marietta College President from 1835-1846) organized a group of people to form a Congregational Church in Harmar. Ground was donated by David Putnam and this church was built on Franklin Street in Harmar. Marietta College students donated a bell to the church. In 1968, the congregation was disbanded and rejoined the First Congregational Church on Front Street. Open Door Baptist Church has held services here for many years.

Putnam Villa/ The Anchorage
403 Harmar Street

Located at the end of Putnam Avenue and overlooking Harmar, this imposing sandstone Italianate style home was built in 1859. John Slocomb, master builder and premier architect, showcased "Putnam Villa" as one of his finest works in the area. The house took ten years to build. The tall tower that fronts the Italianate style house sets an imposing look that can be seen as soon as you cross the Muskingum River. From this vantage point, most of Marietta and its two rivers can be viewed. The walls are made of twenty-four-inch thick sandstone quarried from the hill behind the house. Local oak trees were used for the wood in the twenty-two rooms of the mansion. Broad projecting eaves supported by heavy brackets and narrow paired windows emit a look of wealth and class. The interior boasts of molded plaster chandelier medallions, hand-carved marble fireplaces, and art glass.

Several notable Marietta families enjoyed residing in this home that was a perfect venue for the entertainment of influential people. Douglas and Eliza Putnam commissioned the building of the estate. It is believed that Eliza encouraged her husband, thought to be one of the richest men in Marietta, to build the grand mansion after she returned from a trip to the East. Douglas, son of the well-known early pioneer, David Putnam, was a prominent businessman. He promoted higher education and was secretary of Marietta College from its inception in 1835 until his death in 1894. Putnam signed every diploma during that time!

After the death of Douglas Putnam, the Knox family of Knox Boatyard Company acquired the property. They changed the name of the house to the Anchorage when the driveway was formed in the shape of a ship's anchor. Another resident of the home was Edward MacTaggart, a wealthy oil businessman from Oklahoma, who began to restore the house and furnish it with treasures from his world travels. His sister, Sophia Russell, lived in the house following his death. In the 1960's, the house was converted to a nursing home. In 1996, the Washington County Historical Society acquired the home and began renovations.

The Mill
107 Lancaster Street

With the economic boom of the late 1800's, businessmen often took the opportunity to diversify their interests. George Strecker, a German native, was a boiler maker who conducted his business at 709 Fort Street (now Gilman Avenue). In 1884, he was successful enough to expand his business dealings to construct the mill. The two-story red brick building with slightly arched windows originally housed the business known as Strecker, Tompkins & Co. and operated as a mill and processing plant for grain. Notice the attic and second floor central openings used for plant operations.

The Marietta Milling Company started using the building in 1899. Wheat furnished by farmers was processed at the mill using a modern roller process which could produce one hundred barrels of flour a day. Flour was sold locally and shipped to other markets.

In the early twentieth century, flour production halted and the building had various uses. By 1915, George W. Strecker had sold the building to the U.S. Transfer and Storage Company. Later, the Marietta Distributing Company and the Apex Feed and Supply Company occupied the building. In 1976, the structure was remodeled to be used for office space.

Downtown Marietta
Starting at Front and Greene Streets

Marietta was established to be a model New England-style town in the new frontier. Early leaders surveyed lots, and laid out plans for wide streets and public parks. Streets parallel to the Muskingum River were to be numbered while the cross streets would be named for Revolutionary War officers.

Previous to 1830, Front Street was a commons area with grass, weeds, and some wagon tracks. Putnam Street was mostly residences of prominent citizens. The heart of the town was "The Point," located at the confluence of the Ohio and Muskingum Rivers. The riverfront area of Greene and Ohio Streets was teeming with business and trade, as this was the portal for the vast influx of settlers and goods. The "Flatiron Square" district, as it was called because of the triangular shape of the block, held small shops and dwellings that grew into a great commerce arena. Stores and hotels continued east up river and down to "The Point."

"Flatiron Square" hosted river commerce, hotels and taverns. In time, descendents of the original pioneers found themselves walking alongside people whose language and customs may have differed sharply from their own. Transients would behold Marietta as an oasis in the journey down the Ohio River, making Ohio Street a place of the evening for visitors and some locals. In time, this produced tension and many businesses moved away from the riverfront.

In the mid-1800's, Front Street became a popular business location. With the oil boom of the 1880's and 1890's, the population doubled and the business district exploded with new commerce. With the advent of electricity, railroads, steamships, modern hotels, and entertainment, Marietta's downtown was a welcome spot for business ventures and residency. What visually captures the attention of many people today about Marietta are the remnants of this Victorian heyday.

Bicentennial Plaza
Front and Greene Streets

Bicentennial Plaza was dedicated on July 13, 1987 to mark the two hundredth anniversary of the Ordinance of 1787 (see Westward Expansion Monument) and the two hundredth birthday of Marietta in 1988. The stone column rising out of the water fountain honors the sternwheelers that frequented the Port of Marietta. Incised designs of the feathered smokestacks unique to each of the boats are depicted on the sides of the columns, as well as their dates of service.

The plaza with a fountain of bubbling water is aptly situated on the Ohio River at the Port of Marietta. It is here that early merchants met the sternwheelers that would ply the waters hauling people, goods, mail, and other necessities of life on the frontier. For nearly one hundred years, the port was Marietta's connection to the outside world. This river traffic enabled Marietta to grow and prosper as flatboats, packets, and sternwheelers came into port. The original stones used to secure the bank are still embedded in the ground of the public landing. Each September, Marietta hosts the Sternwheel Festival for a weekend of entertainment and, of course, a sternwheel race on Sunday. Sternwheeler enthusiasts bring their paddlewheelers of all sizes to line the riverbank for a step back into a time when rivers were the highways.

Picketed Point
Marker on the west end of parking lot near the Lafayette Hotel

The land on the east side of the confluence of the Muskingum and Ohio Rivers was the site of Picketed Point, the long-awaited land that the first pioneers established as their "town." Within five days of their arrival in April of 1788, the settlers had cleared four acres of land. Indians warned that the land often flooded, but the settlers ignored their warning. Settlers built tents, temporary dwellings, cabins, small businesses, and prepared fields with corn, potatoes, and beans. On June 5th, James Mitchell Varnum, one of the first territorial judges of the Northwest Territory, arrived with forty settlers, including James Owen and his wife, Mary, the first woman to settle here.

With all the preparations the Ohio Company of Associates had made for their new town, it is surprising that a name had not been decided. Initially, the men at the "Point" called it "Muskingum," a name taken from the Delaware Indian word, *mooskingung*, meaning elk eye river. Manasseh Cutler, who negotiated with the Confederation Congress on behalf of the Ohio Company to purchase the land, preferred the Greek word, "Adelphia," meaning brethren. By July of 1788, the name Marietta was decided in order to honor the French Queen Marie Antoinette who had assisted the colonies in achieving independence.

In 1791, a stockade of pickets was erected on the west and north sides of the "point" for fear of attack during the Ohio Indian War. By this time, Picketed Point had become a business district and about 20 families had taken up residency. This area had the first tavern, the first hotel, the first post office, and the first rental property of the Northwest Territory.

While walking around in the parking lot, notice other historical markers.

The Gay Nineties In Marietta

Much of what gives Marietta its ambiance today is credited to the burst of construction of homes and businesses of the 1880's through the early 1900's. If you look at the design of the downtown buildings, the date and name of the structure often appears near the roof. Sometimes the structure is crowned with Victorian flourishes, or the architecture of the second and third floors is cast in symmetrical rows of double-hung windows with rounded lintels. Don't forget to look up as you enjoy the streets of Marietta.

In American history, the Gay Nineties was often remembered as a time of invention, prosperity of industrialists, and investments. However, the decade was burdened with economic depression, including the Panic of 1883, widespread unemployment, the closing of banks and railroads, and strikes by workers. Unlike some towns in the United States, Marietta prospered during this time.

A major reason Marietta's economy thrived was due to the development of local oil and natural gas finds in southeastern Ohio and nearby West Virginia. In the early days, the greasy ooze would frustrate people searching for salt. "Seneca Oil", named after the Indian tribe who often traded it, was used as medicine. In the field, oil was undervalued and often discarded, even though it was found in sufficient quantities at nearby Duck Creek and Macksburg. As stated in the *Century Review of Marietta*, famed local historian and scientist Dr. Hildreth predicted in 1826 that oil and natural gas "will be used soon for lighting the streets of Ohio cities." By the 1860's, the value of oil and natural gas was realized and Marietta would become the hub of the industry. By 1900, more than twenty companies in Marietta were directly related to the oil and natural gas industry.

Farmers at Train Station on Second Street.
Courtesy of Washington County Historical Society

Downtown Marietta flourished with commerce by the turn of the twentieth century. The affluence of the 1890's brought about immense opportunity for businesses of all kinds. Florists, clothiers, bakers, bookbinders, milliners, jewelers, dressmakers, and tailors of

Bellevue Hotel Postcard.
Courtesy of Washington County Historical Society

gentlemen's fine suits were all in demand. Merchants no longer just provided staples. Stores marketed services and provisions for a finer, cultural life. For example, Miss M. Eno Brown advertised her Modern Hair Dressing and Manicuring Parlor, where hair could be properly dressed for receptions, balls, parties, and the theater. A portrait could be made at the Ideal Art Studio, a Turkish bath could be enjoyed at the Marietta Sanitarium, and clothing could be taken to the Chinese laundry. The India Spice and Drug Company provided seasonings for refined culinary tastes, and Styer's Sarsaparilla store served beverages and a blood purifier for good health. Saloons then called sample rooms offered a free lunch with the purchase of beer. Marietta catered the finer accouterments to the ladies and gentlemen of the community in ways accustomed for people in larger cities.

Big business expanded the commercial district with the construction of large brick or stone buildings that replaced some of the smaller framed structures. Otto Brothers Department Store and the Strecker Brothers Company, one of the largest saddlery manufacturers in the United States, opened huge stores in the relatively new business area of Putnam Street. Entrepreneurs found enough confidence in the economy to add two new financial institutions in 1889: Citizens National Bank and the German National Bank. The Marietta Chair Company, the Nye Stove Foundry, and the Knox Boatyard employed enough workers to meet the pressing needs of southeastern Ohio. Increased industries allowed for wholesale grocers, such as Penrose & Simpson on Front Street and Worrall Grocery on Second Street, to establish businesses that could reach outside of the city. Southeastern Ohio was well-known for its agricultural goods that were transported by the railroads. Horse-drawn wagons, ladened with fruits and vegetables to be shipped to other cities, queued at the depot on Second Street. Marietta boasted of nearly ten downtown hotels. The St. Cloud Hotel, rebuilt in brick by Elizabeth Cisler Gross in 1890, was known as one of the finest in southeastern Ohio. Traveling businessmen and visitors lodged in modern accommodations with a first-rate dining room for only a dollar per day. The St. Cloud Hotel and the heralded St. James Hotel, both near Front and Butler, were conveniently located close to the railroad depot. The impressive, modern Bellevue Hotel, known for having one of the first elevators in the area, overlooked the scenic Ohio River and drew lodgers arriving daily by steamboats. With material comforts in demand and cash flowing, Marietta's growth was at a prospering peak.

As a part of the culture of Marietta, people of Anglo-Saxon heritage had proudly held leadership and wealth in the city. With the arrival of more diverse immigrants, a multicultural flavor was evident in businesses and society. The population of Marietta more than doubled between 1880 and 1900. Even though African-Americans had always been in Marietta, their numbers increased in the 1890's. Chinese, American Indians, the French, the Irish, Syrians, Jews, Italians, and others added to the cultural flavor in Marietta near the turn of the century, but the majority of immigrants were from Germany. Favoring the rich farmland, Germans settled in Washington County as early as the 1830's.

Syrian immigrants on Tiber Way.
Courtesy of Washington County HIstorical Society

In time, Germans in Marietta held jobs in a variety of businesses: leatherworkers, dry goods dealers, grocers, shoemakers, saloonkeepers, cigar makers, bakers, and brewers. Germans, known for thriftiness and hard work, were respected in business matters, but they retained their German culture in social groups, churches, and language. Germans owned many of the successful Marietta businesses of the 1890's. Even though Marietta was touted as a town developed by the descendents of New England pioneers, German contributions to the growth of the city were significant.

Marietta's centennial celebration of 1888 served as a catalyst for many citizens to show pride in the accomplishments of the past and promote a vision of the prospering future. Prominent leaders dedicated the 1890's to promoting the transformation of an old frontier town into a modern city. With forethought, they took advantage of new technology and modern practices to create an infrastructure to match the burst of economic prosperity. Dirt streets were bricked, eliminating clouds of dust and the mud-splattered clothing and carriages. The waterworks system replaced many cisterns in town to provide sanitary drinking water, even though some residents disliked the taste. Members of the fire department were no longer volunteers, and had modern equipment to fight the fires that plagued the city. Citizens who had become wary of the transients in town welcomed new electric streetlights. Lighted steel arches spanning Front Street were the crown jewels of the business district. Horse-drawn streetcars were replaced with electric streetcars and railways that connected Marietta from within and to nearby communities. A city hall and auditorium, reserved for entertainment, was remodeled in 1894 with the auditorium enlarged to hold fifteen hundred people. Concern for the good health of the community led to the opening of Grace Hospital in 1899 and the Marietta Sanitarium for treatment of chronic disease in 1900. The city expanded outward to form suburbs, such as the Norwood subdivision, platted for development of cottages and businesses. In the early 1900's, four railways and the Williamstown Bridge across the Ohio River linked Marietta to Cincinnati, Columbus, Zanesville, and Parkersburg, West Virginia. Four newspapers were published locally, including the *Marietta Zeitung* printed in German. In little over a decade, Marietta proudly showed a face of progress fitting to welcome the advent of the twentieth century. During this time, Marietta grew up to take its place as a modern, prosperous city.

Knox Boatyard Flourished in Late 1800's
Courtesy of Washington County Historical Society

Lafayette Hotel
101 Front Street

The confluence of the Ohio and Muskingum Rivers has been the center of activity since the first pioneers of the Ohio Company of Associates built cabins on this land in 1788. Business boomed in Marietta by the 1890's, and the stylish and modern Bellevue Hotel, built in 1892, flourished on this corner. The distinctive, onion-domed turret overlooked the busy dock of the town. Unfortunately, fire destroyed a large portion of the hotel in 1916.

In 1918, local businessmen used part of the remaining Bellevue structure to build the Lafayette Hotel, named to honor the 1825 visit of Marquis de Lafayette, the French hero of the American Revolution. Throughout the years, the hotel has had additions, renovations, and several owners. S. Durward Hoag, the famed residential owner for many years, was instrumental in the hotel's success and was an active member of the community. Hoag was a painter, photographer, newspaper columnist, and city councilman. One of his most important contributions to the city was convincing Washington D. C. authorities to route Interstate 77 through Marietta, thus ensuring further growth of the city. He loved the town and loved entertaining people in his home, the hotel that he personally decorated. The hotel restaurant, The Gun Room, contains a fine display of artifacts such as a collection of handcrafted long rifles, a boat's telegraph, steamboat instruments, and pilot wheels. The Grand Ballroom hosts music, special events, and conventions. The Riverview Lounge, open since 1934 under various names, allows patrons to overlook the Ohio River and watch the traffic of commercial barges and pleasure craft.

Schafer Building
140 Front Street

The Schafer Leather Store is the oldest, continuously family-owned business in Marietta. Five generations of Schafers have operated the leather business since 1865. For most of that time, 140 Front Street has been home to the Schafer family.

Louis Schaefer came to America from Germany with his parents and two older brothers in 1855. He became an apprentice to Jacob Ebinger in the harness business in 1860. During the Civil War, he worked in a government harness shop in Cincinnati where he gained enough experience, upon his return, to open A & L Saddlery with his brother, Adam, in Harmar.

In 1860, the brothers moved the business to 140 Front, a framed building owned by Maria Woodbridge. However, in 1884, a devastating flood destroyed the building. Louis, on his own, purchased the land, built the present building, changed the spelling of his name, and renamed the store, Louis Schafer. It housed the harness business and two offices on the second floor. In the 1890's he was joined in business by his two sons, Louis P. and Frank. The business expanded to include small leather goods, such as trunks and traveling bags.

In 1925, Louis P. Schafer succeeded his father as sole owner. His son, Robert L., joined the family business about 1934 when the country was reeling from the Great Depression. The business was also troubled because of the decline in use of harnesses. In 1945, Robert became the sole owner, then shared the business with his son, Robert Jr., who succeeded him in 1968. In the 1970's, the original building was expanded with the addition of a storeroom and receiving room. Marilyn Schafer and son, Robert H. purchased an adjoining building, opened the interior with the original store, and added the western shop. Robert H. Schafer, owner since 1994, has enjoyed the revitalization of Front Street in recent years.

Flood Markers
On right side of Schafer building

Marietta has had a history of notable floods. Stand in front of the Schafer building and look on the southern side of the second story. White markers show the water level of Marietta's highest floods. The brown marker at street level shows the level of water in 2004 when hurricane Ivan brought stormy weather.

When the first pioneers began building their dwellings at "Picketed Point," local Indians cautioned them about flooding in the area. They pointed to debris left in the trees from the last high water, but the pioneers continued building at the confluence of the Muskingum and Ohio Rivers. The rivers were vitally important for trade and transportation, so the town stayed near the river and was repeatedly flooded from time to time.

In 1790, two years after arriving, the pioneers experienced the first recorded high water. The first significant flood in 1813 brought 8 feet of water onto Front Street. The winter weather brought thick chunks of ice crashing into buildings and damaging fences and orchards. The city lost about twenty buildings in the flood of 1832. One building, the fire engine house, drifted out into the Ohio River eventually making its way to Louisville, Kentucky. A bizarre weather change caused the third highest flood in early 1884. The middle of January brought a foot of snow. Within a month, the temperature warmed to 70 degrees, melted the snow, and brought rain. The rivers swelled quickly.

The worst natural disaster in the state of Ohio occurred in 1913 and Marietta was not spared. Almost all of downtown was under water, with 120 homes lost and 200 off the foundations. The 1937 flood covered nearly half the city with 8 to 16 feet of water.

The Ohio River Museum has more information on floods in Marietta and a display of high water markers.

The Register Building
177 Front Street

Every prospering community required a locally printed news source. In 1801, *The Ohio Gazette Territorial and Virginia Herald* appeared in Marietta as a local weekly newspaper. The press was made of wood with a stone bed. For $2.00 a year, a person could read four pages of national and foreign news with legal advertisements. Interest in the power of the press during the 1800's fueled at least ten papers in Marietta, published with various levels of success.

The Register Building, as it was called, was built in 1888 to replace a plant that had been lost to fire. The *Marietta Register* office was in the rear of this three-story building that was equipped with printing presses to distribute the eight-page newspaper. In the prosperous last years of the century, there were four other newspapers printed in Marietta: *Marietta Times, Marietta Leader, Marietta Zeitung* (German), and the *Marietta Daily Leader.*

In 1900, it was not uncommon for several businesses to share a single building. The Marietta Bookstore, the first bookseller in Marietta, shared the first floor with the Oil Well Supply Company. Headquartered in Pittsburgh, the Marietta store opened in 1890 at the beginning of the oil and natural gas boom. It kept supplies for oil and gas wells, pipelines, refineries, steam, gas, and water plants. The second floor held businesses and the third floor was home to the Knights of Pythias, a social society.

D. B. Anderson Jr. Building
197 Front Street

The Victorian style building at the corner of Front and Butler was situated in one of the busiest areas at the turn of the century in historic Marietta. Behind it was the St. James Hotel, and across the street was the prestigious St. Cloud Hotel. The main railroad line paralleled all three businesses. The D. B. Anderson Jr. building's angular lines forming the edges of the roof, the rich color of the brick, and the large windows allowing for the Victorian Era daylight were all classic designs for success.

The first practical jeweler of Marietta was D. B. Anderson who opened a store at Front and Ohio Streets in 1817. He was also considered to be Marietta's first clock maker. His son, D.B. Jr., assumed the business in a shop near Front and Monroe Streets in 1854. Watches, clocks, and jewelry were sold and repaired as well as eyeglasses and spectacles. In 1883, Anderson erected this building and opened Pioneer Jewelry at 197 Front Street. A local paper of the 1880's, the *Marietta Register* stated, "The building is an ornament to the street, and the store a valuable addition to the business interests of the city." Unfortunately, the same year, floodwaters reached the building. Bricks were placed on the exterior of the building to record the high water levels. Following Anderson's retirement, A. B. Regnier, grandson of D. B. Anderson Jr., operated as a jeweler and optician. The family business in this building closed in 1911 when Sarah Elizabeth Anderson made an indenture contract with Fred Augenstein, who opened a barbershop.

Monument Of The 48 Pioneers
Intersection of Front and Butler Streets

In August of 1787, the directors of the Ohio Company of Associates met at the "Bunch of Grapes" tavern near Boston, Massachusetts to hear that Rev. Manasseh Cutler had attained over a million acres of land for them in the Ohio Country from the federal government. Later, the decision was made that the party would consist of 48 men, including four surveyors, one blacksmith, six boat builders, four house carpenters, nine laborers, and other assistants.

The first party of men traveled seven weeks, reaching Simeral's Ferry in southwestern Pennsylvania in January. The second party, led by General Rufus Putnam, joined them in February. Boat building began under the leadership of Captain Jonathan Devol, with the largest named the "Adventure Galley" which was later changed to the "Mayflower" in honor of the first settlers of Massachusetts. On April 1, the group departed from Simeral's Ferry (now West Newton, Pennsylvania). After six days on the Ohio River, the group arrived at Fort Harmar on April 7. According to some reports, Return Jonathan Meigs, Sr. rode a horse over the distance instead of traveling by boat.

It is reported that the boats overshot the intended shore of the east bank of the Muskingum and were welcomed by the soldiers of the fort. Later these men helped the pioneers to the correct landing site. Native Americans of the Delaware and Wyandotte tribes led by Chief Captain Pipe were also on hand to greet the pioneers.

Lock Keeper's House
243 Front Street

Before the construction of highways and railroads, navigable rivers were the main arteries for transportation of people, goods, mail, and entertainment. Rivers were not dependable, however, because summer water levels were too shallow for boat traffic and the spring rains made the water too high and fast. To connect communities in southeastern Ohio, eleven locks and dams were constructed in the Muskingum River from Marietta to Dresden in 1841. The locks were built so one person could hand operate the doors in fifteen minutes, allowing boats to pass. This was considered an engineering feat. The lock house in Marietta was built in 1899 at a cost of $3,500 on land worth $12,000. Since the locks operated twenty-four hours a day, the lockmaster and his family lived on site. Shipbuilding in Marietta boomed and the river traffic was good for commerce up and down the river. Unfortunately, as a result of the 1913 flood, many locks and dams were closed. Additionally, with the construction of highways and transportation with trucks, the great need for the operation of locks and dams diminished. Marietta's dam was removed in 1968, but the lock house remains as a part of our history.

The unique design of the house lends flavor to the Marietta waterfront. The lock house, constructed of brick, shows Dutch influence in the architecture with the stepped gables in the front and rear. Bands of decorative tile with different designs encircle the house. The tile in the rear gable facing the Muskingum River remains intact, but the front gable has lost the tiles.

Old Post Office
100 Putnam Street

Private messengers carried Marietta's early mail. The first official postal service for Marietta was established in 1794 in a two-story log store building at the confluence of the Muskingum and Ohio Rivers. A regular route linking new frontier towns with the original thirteen states was opened, with mail transported on the Ohio River between Pittsburgh and Cincinnati. Return Jonathon Meigs, Jr., the first postmaster, received mail every two weeks in Marietta. In 1798, the first route opened between Marietta and Zanesville: it required two to four days. Later, an overland mail route was developed to link Marietta, Athens, and Cincinnati. In these early days, the post office was housed at several locations. This building at the corner of Putnam and Front Streets may have been constructed as early as 1806 and utilized as the Marietta Post Office from 1819 to 1853.

The old Post Office is considered to be the oldest existing commercial building in Marietta. The Georgian-style building was constructed as a three-story building. The first floor housed the post office, a notions store, and a reading room that supplied out-of-town newspapers. The American Union Lodge No. 1 met on the second floor, and the third floor was a school for men in the study of Greek and Latin. When the streets were raised as a flood control measure, the first floor became the basement. The Post Office was moved to the St. Clair building around 1900. Between 1913 and 1938, display windows on the current first floor were installed. For many years, the building was used as a drug store.

Bank Of Marietta
101 Putnam Street

When early pioneers experienced economic growth, prominent members of the community established a financial institution. The Bank of Marietta was chartered on February 10, 1808. Banking business was conducted in the home of David Putnam on the west side of the Muskingum River. In 1813, the bank moved to the east side of the river to a one-story brick building north of the Congregational Church on Front Street. In 1833, it was moved again to this newly-built Greek Revival style building at the corner of Front and Putnam Streets. This stately building of the 1830's had a symmetrical-shaped front, including the pediment with heavy cornice and the wide, plain frieze. The front central pilasters, columns, and narrow windows around the door are typical for the style of architecture. The Bank of Marietta had a built-in vault and a residence for its cashier on the second story. The charter for the bank expired in 1843.

Steady growth in business in the second half of the nineteenth century spurred the need for several financial institutions. In the 1850's, the Bank of Exchange opened and, in 1864, the First National Bank of Marietta was chartered. After the Civil War, other financial institutions began to open. In the latter part of the century, businesses flourished, providing the need and capital for new banks. The following banks/building & loans were open for business by the late 1890's: The Dime Savings Society, Citizens National Bank, the German National Bank, The Washington County Savings, The Pioneer City Building & Loan Company, and the German Savings Building and Loan Company.

First Congregational Church
318 Front Street

As a part of the design for the Northwest Territory's first city, the building of a church was among the top priorities. Early pioneers observed Sunday services at both Campus Martius and in Munsell's Hall at Picketed Point. The First Congregational Church was organized in 1796 with Daniel Story serving as the pastor. Services were also held at the Muskingum Academy building, erected in 1798, until the congregation moved into their permanent location. In 1809, a frame church with twin towers patterned after the Hollis Street Congregational Church in Boston was built on Front Street. The structure cost $7,300. It became a landmark for river men who called it the "Two Horned Church." During the reform movement of the nineteenth century, Congregationalists supported creating an improved moral atmosphere by holding at least twelve revivals between 1840 and 1869.

In 1901, remodeling began on the church with the addition of a gabled extension supported by pillars. The frame church lasted for nearly one hundred years until it was destroyed by fire in 1905. A new structure, similar in architecture using yellow brick, was built on the old site. In 1928, a spacious parish hall was added in the rear. In 1957, Congregational denominations merged nationally to form the United Church of Christ. The church today celebrates over two hundred years of continuing worship, making it the longest lasting congregation in Marietta.

Return Jonathan Meigs, Jr. Home
326 Front Street

As citizens of the first settlement in the Northwest Territory, many men had the vision to establish themselves in the political world of the young frontier. Return Jonathan Meigs, Jr., was the son of a prominent Ohio Company Associate, and graduated from Yale. Meigs, a successful lawyer and merchant, placed his heart in politics and devoted his time to establish law and order in the new frontier. He was the first postmaster of Marietta (1794-1795), a Judge of the Northwest Territory (1798), Chief Judge of the Ohio Supreme Court (1803-1804), U.S. Senator (1808-1810), fourth Governor of Ohio (1810-1814), and Postmaster General of the United States under President Madison and President Monroe (1814-1823). He played a major role in the War of 1812 while governor. Fort Meigs near Maumee, Ohio, and the county of Meigs were named to honor him.

The Meigs home was considered one of the most elegant houses in Marietta. Meigs, a tall man with a striking appearance, was known for his intelligence and leadership. The home was well furnished, including the first Brussels carpet in town and a "hair-cloth" sofa that was considered quite showy at the time. The Governor and Mrs. Meigs would ride about in a very handsome carriage, but when traveling to the capital, both would ride horseback, with Mrs. Meigs's party dresses crushed into saddle bags. The house saw much entertainment, especially when Mary, their daughter, was of the age to entertain suitors.

The Federal style house regally stands on a slight rise overlooking Muskingum Park. Construction began in 1802 and was completed within three years. Typical of the style are the symmetrical placement of the windows topped by double keystone lintels and the striking string course separating the two- story building. In 1854, a portico, balcony, and wrought iron fence were added. In 1916-1917, a side porch and back rooms were added. The house was centered on the lot, raised six feet to guard against high water, and moved twenty-five feet back from the street. Notice that the lower courses of bricks are newer due to this move.

Start Westward Monument
East Muskingum Park on Front Street

In 1938, the Monument to the Start Westward, sometimes called the "Westward Ho" monument, was dedicated by President Franklin D. Roosevelt. Nearly 100,000 people turned out to see the president. The monument was to honor the one hundredth and fiftieth year anniversary of the Ordinance of 1787 and the opening of the Northwest Territory. It was designed by Gutzon Borglum of Mount Rushmore fame. The installation consists of three men standing on a rock, with a rowboat and two men and one woman behind them. It represents the first landing of pioneers and the beginning of U.S. expansion beyond the Allegheny region. Arthur St. Clair was inaugurated at this site as the first governor of the Northwest Territory.

The Ordinance of 1787 was created under the Articles of Confederation, the basis of government prior to the U.S. Constitution, on July 1787. The major reason for the document was to bring order to the newly-acquired lands north and west of the Ohio River, particularly to ensure the land would be used for creation of new states. The ordinance listed the following provisions: 1) established a plan for admission of new states, 2) established a territorial government, 3) established land parcels that were set aside for education and ministry, 4) provided for the prohibition of slavery, and 5) established civil rights (religious tolerance, right of habeas corpus, bans on excessive fines, prohibition of cruel and unusual punishment).

Buckley House
332 Front Street

The Woodbridge House, as it was originally called, was built in 1879 in the name of Maria Woodbridge, granddaughter of the first storeowner in Marietta. Her father, Dudley Woodbridge Jr., a Yale graduate, was an influential mercantile businessman who was also active in politics and shipbuilding.

Maria suffered a life-long physical weakness as a result of a spinal injury caused by a fall in childhood. It was likely that she experienced chronic pain. Maria was the first president of a society in Marietta called "The Musical Union" and was a charter member of the Marietta Reading Club. Interestingly, history tells us there was a suicide in the house. Maria had a German maid who fell in love with a Chinese Marietta Academy student who was boarding at the Woodbridge residence. They knelt and pledged their love in a Chinese marriage tradition. Upon learning of the love affair, Maria sent the maid to Cincinnati and chastised the young man. Overwhelmed with grief, he said goodbye to friends, dressed for burial, and went to his bed with a bottle of chloroform. According to local legend, his spirit still walks on the second floor!

The Victorian Period house with a two-tiered porch shows a Southern influence. Notice the heights of the banisters on the two porches. The first floor banister is designed lower so not to block the view of the river. It is called the Buckley House because this family resided there for more than fifty years. It has been a bed and breakfast and a restaurant.

Shipman House
404 Front Street

This Front Street house was built in 1834 for the Rev. Luther G. Bingham, pastor of the First Congregational Church. In 1830, Bingham formed the Institute of Education that included a high school and ladies' seminary. Within two years, the Institute's enrollment was two hundred thirty pupils, half of which came from the states of New York, Vermont, Massachusetts, Pennsylvania, Maryland, Kentucky, and Virginia. Prominent community members acknowledged the institution as a way to build Marietta's cultural reputation and, thus, sought a charter for a public college. From this early Institute of Education, Marietta College was born and chartered in 1835 to give degrees. Soon after, Rev. Bingham moved to Cincinnati and the house was sold to his son-in-law, Samuel Shipman.

Samuel, then a partner with his older brother, Charles, had a dry goods business on Greene Street. He was a deacon at the First Congregational Church for thirty-eight years, treasurer of Marietta College from 1856-1867, and trustee for the college until his death in 1880. The house had several owners after Shipman, including Marietta College professor Thomas D. Biscoe, husband of Mary Ellen Shipman, Samuel's youngest daughter.

This Greek Revival style house has had a rear frame addition, a side brick addition, and a rounding of the porch. In the 1940's, this single-family house was divided into apartments and later converted into offices. Cawley & People's Funeral Home joined this home to the Holden House to expand their business in the late 1970's.

Holden House
408 Front Street

Rev. Luther Bingham owned this lot that he sold to William Holden in 1840. William was the oldest son of Joseph Holden, an early merchant who had come to Marietta in 1803 from Massachusetts. William joined his father's business and later formed the W., J., & J. Holden firm with his two brothers, Joseph, Jr. and James. In the early days, the store acted informally as a political headquarters for the Whigs and was frequently termed "Uncle Joe Holden's Senate." It was located at the corner of Greene and Front. William retired in 1843 and Joseph, Jr. left the business in 1857, leaving it solely to James.

When William died, Maria Trevor, his sister, acquired the lot and sold it to her brother James. An early building was lost or damaged shortly before 1853 when James Holden built the present brick house with twelve-inch-thick walls and twelve-foot-high ceilings. The Federal style house retains a rectangular shape with symmetrically placed windows and a low-pitched gable roof.

After the death of James Holden in 1899, the house had a variety of owners that took up residency. But in 1966, it was purchased to be used as a funeral home. In the mid-1990's, Cawley and People's Funeral Home joined the Holden house with the Shipman house to enlarge the business.

Ohio River Museum
W. P. Snyder, Jr.
601 Front Street

The Ohio River Museum opened in 1974 on the banks of the Muskingum River. The facility has three exhibit buildings featuring the origins and natural history of the Ohio River, the history of steamboats on the Ohio River, and boat building from the steamboat era. It also has the extensive collection of the Sons & Daughters of Pioneer Rivermen.

Of special interest when visiting the museum is the steamboat, the *W. P. Snyder, Jr.*, the last intact steam-powered "pool type" sternwheeled towboat in the United States. Originally named the *W. H. Clingerman*, it was built as a Carnegie Steel Company towboat in Pittsburgh in 1918. Later, it was called the *J. L. Perry* and then the *A-1*. In September 1945, it was sold to the Crucible Steel Company of Pittsburgh, Pennsylvania and named the *W. P. Snyder, Jr.* The boat was used to tow coal on the Monongahela River until 1953. In 1955, the Ohio Historical Society acquired it to exhibit at the Ohio River Museum. It was the last steamboat to go through Lock #1 in Marietta before that lock and dam were removed. Captain Fred Way docked the *W. P. Snyder, Jr.* in its final resting place at the museum on September 16, 1955.

Marietta Brewing Company
Second and St. Clair Streets

Halfway along St. Clair Street is an alley called Old Brewery Lane. With a few remnants of original buildings, the marker is almost the only remaining memory of German beer-making at the Second Street location. Between 1866 and 1876, Union Brewery operated on the corner under several different owners. The brewery was sold at auction, eventually coming into the hands of John Schneider, who ran a successful business until he died in 1884. His wife, Elizabeth, and sons continued production until 1890, then closed the plant and became saloon owners.

In 1898, three German immigrants, William Feller, August V. Kuehn, and Jacob Epple bought the old Union Brewery. They improved the plant by adding a bottling house, an ice plant, and other modern machinery. It was renamed the Marietta Brewery and with a crew of twenty workers successfully produced 8,000-12,000 barrels of beer a year. In 1903, Feller left the business and August V. Kuehn became the president, his son, George, the secretary/treasurer, and Epple, the vice president. The newly incorporated Marietta Brewing Company continued the sale of beer in town and the nearby communities as well as along the Ohio River.

Across the nation, the Temperance Movement increasingly pushed for prohibition. In 1908, under pressure from the local temperance chapter, the Rose Law passed, resulting in the temporary closure of the brewery. The law stated alcohol could not be sold; however, it could be made. In 1911, the brewery resumed bottling with a market in Parkersburg, West Virginia. After Kuehn's death in 1914, Jacob Epple became president and his wife, Minnie, served as vice-president. Production continued until federal Prohibition came in 1919. The Marietta Brewery/Brewing Company was the longest lasting beer-making establishment in the area at that time. Today, the site is a medical building that uses part of the original stone beer cellar as a unique physical therapy room. The large red brick building on the other side of the alley was also a part of the original brewery operations.

Campus Martius Museum
601 Second Street

Campus Martius Museum preserves two of the oldest buildings in Marietta and the Northwest Territory: the Rufus Putnam House and the Ohio Land Office. With the opening of the Northwest Territory, Native Americans grew more wary and restless, so the settlers of Marietta built Campus Martius. The fort was named after the plain adjacent to ancient Rome, the word meaning "Field of War." It was designed as a square of dwellings with the outside walls forming the stockade. Each of the four corners held a blockhouse. Though never attacked, the fortification was used for about ten years. The Rufus Putnam House was never moved from its present original location and the museum was built to enclose it. The Ohio Land Office was moved from its original location to the yard of the museum. Both buildings are listed on the Register of Historic Places.

General Rufus Putnam has been given credit as the person responsible for the early settlement of Marietta. He was an able engineer in the continental army throughout the Revolutionary War. His design of West Point on the Hudson River prevented the use of the river by the British forces. General Rufus Putnam was the leader of the Ohio Company of Associates, a group of war veterans from New England who settled Marietta in 1788. The purchase contract was for 1,500,000 acres of land at a cost of approximately eight and one-half cents per acre. As leader of the Ohio Company, Putnam helped to set up the local government and sell parcels of land to new settlers from the Ohio Land Office, the first "real estate" company and the oldest building in the territory. From 1796 to 1803, Putnam served the nation as Surveyor General of the United States.

Campus Martius Museum welcomes visitors to stroll through the Rufus Putnam home and Ohio Land Office and to explore the three floors of exhibits. History comes alive with the museum's numerous original artifacts depicting the life and culture of settlement in Marietta. Other exhibits include the presence of prehistoric Indian activity in the area and migration of white settlers to Ohio and the Northwest Territory.

Ohio River Sternwheel Festival. *Photo by Karen Spencer*

Front Street. *Photo by Karen Spencer*

Sternwheel Paddles
Photo by Shila Wilson

W.P. Snyder, Jr.
Photo by Karen Spencer

100 Block of Front Street
Photo by Karen Spencer

Petunia Baskets Line Streets in the Summer
Photo by Karen Spencer

Barge on the Ohio River
Photo by Karen Spencer

Horse Carriage
Photo by Larry Hall

Harmar Village
Photo by Shila Wilson

100 Block of Front Street
Photo by Shila Wilson

Walking Across the Harmar
Railroad Bridge
Photo by Shila Wilson

Mound Cemetery
Photo by Shila Wilson

East Muskingum Park and River Trail
Photo by Jann Adams

Harmar Bridge
Photo by Jann Adams

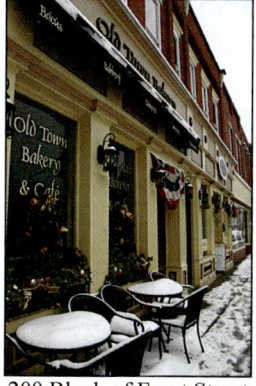

200 Block of Front Street
Photo by Shila Wilson

Brick Sidewalk from 1800's
Photo by Karen Spencer

200 Block of Front Street
Photo on left by Jann Adams, photo on right Shila Wilson

Resident Geese at Ohio River Levee
Photo by Jann Adams

Harmar Village Scene
Photo by Jann Adams

Moon Over Marietta
Photo by Shila Wilson

Sacra Via Park

From Front Street to Fourth Street along Sacra Via Street and Warren Street

Long before the Delaware and Tuscarawas Indians settled in the Muskingum River Valley, prehistoric people had built earthworks and mounds on nearly one hundred acres in southeastern Ohio. It was with great foresight that the early settlers enacted resolutions to preserve these unusual areas as public places. The sites in Marietta were the first of Ohio's prehistoric Indian earthworks to be surveyed, mapped, and described.

Sacra Via Park earthworks have been attributed to the Hopewell Culture that dates back to as early as 100 BCE and as late as 500 CE. It is believed to be a ceremonial center. Originally, the park was enclosed by earthen walls on each side leading from the Muskingum River to a large square area that included the platform mound on Fourth Street. This mound was given the Latin name, Quadranaou, by early settlers. In 1843, the earthen walls were removed and the clay was used by brick makers for local buildings.

The block containing the mound is also referred to as Camp Tupper, as the square was used during the Civil War as an encampment for soldiers. It was named for Major Anselm Tupper, commander of Campus Martius during the Indian War of the 1790's. Tupper, one of the original pioneers to arrive in 1788, was the first schoolteacher of Marietta and the Northwest Territory. Respected and well-liked, Anselm Tupper showed great diversity of interest, being a poet, classical scholar, a surveyor, and an adventurer. Interestingly, Anselm Tupper was the second officer of the vessel *Orlando*, built at Marietta in 1803, which sailed from Marietta down the Ohio, the Mississippi, across the Atlantic, through the Mediterranean, and to Adriatic Sea. He then returned home to Marietta.

B. E. Stoehr House
701 Fifth Street

This beautiful Queen Anne style house rests in the "Hilltop Dutch" area, as it was called during a period of German immigration to Marietta. Many Germans lived and farmed in the area north of Warren Street. This red brick house stands out among the other frame houses in the neighborhood. The style is complete with its rounded tower, heavy stone lintels and sills. The front stone arched window on the front porch is highlighted with stain glass.

B.E. Stoehr, a native of Germany, arrived in Marietta in 1860 as a brewer. He boarded with Mrs. C. Gaddens, one of only two brewers in town making common beer. Stoehr was the first to make lager beer and is lauded as the first German brewer in Marietta, though it is likely small sample rooms in Marietta had their own "house" recipes. In 1871, Stoehr had a saloon on Second Street. The large brick house was built about 1897 for the Stoehr family. Several lots were owned showing the residence, a sample room, a bottling works, and carriage house near the corner of Fifth and Warren Streets. In 1902, B.E. Stoehr was an Agent for the Christian Moerlein Brewing Company of Cincinnati. Stoehr received shipments by way of the railroad, had an icehouse for cold storage, filled orders, and made deliveries by wagon or railroad. He bottled his own beer and it is said he had a beer garden in the yard for friends and patrons.

Washington County Library
615 Fifth Street

The 1796 private library of Colonel Israel Putnam could be considered the first library of the Northwest Territory. Later, the collection would become the origin of the Belpre Farmers Library. In 1836, the Marietta Library Association was formed under the leadership of John Mills, a prominent businessman. The association collected funds through the sale of five-dollar shares and increased its collections.

Donations helped to build the first library in the 300 block of Front Street where the Masonic Temple now stands. The Civil War Era ushered in a serious decline in library use, since people became more interested in current events in newspapers at newsstands. Library Hall, as it was called, became more of a lecture hall and meeting place. For example, the Anti-Slavery Society met there and the city council held meetings in the building until 1870 when city hall was built. The library closed in 1883, but after a few years, the association persisted in organizing a library, first in the St. Clair building on Putnam Street, and then in the high school on Scammel Street.

With the financial assistance of Andrew Carnegie, funds enabled the Library Association to build a permanent library in 1913. The prehistoric Hopewell platform mound called Capitolium on Fifth Street was offered as the site. The brick and limestone structure designed by George Hovey was completed in 1918.

Larchmont
524 Second Street

High off the street and secluded by trees, this three-story white painted brick Greek Revival style house holds a mysteriously unique history. Based on the original owner's journal, the house was begun around 1834, even though it was not recorded until 1840. Albigence Waldo Putnam, a lawyer and grandson of Colonel Israel Putnam of Belpre, had the house built after he married his second wife, Cornelia Virginia Sevier. However, the Putnams never lived there. In 1839, they bought land near Nashville, Tennessee and moved into a home called "Waverly Place." Family legend surmises that Mrs. Putnam, daughter of the governor of the southern state of Tennessee, refused to come to the north because she could not bring her slave to the free state of Ohio.

The orphaned mansion has hosted many occupants, some who stayed longer than others. Colonel Augustus Stone, a Harmar businessman active in the local militia, had supervised the construction of Larchmont. He was married to Putnam's sister Charlotte and, when A. W. Putnam decided not to return to Marietta, the Stones moved into the house. Perhaps it was because of Stone's abolitionist interest that the house was rumored to be a station on the Underground Railroad, but this is unsubstantiated. For unknown reasons, the Stones moved out and the building was leased to the St. John's (Episcopal) Female Academy, a finishing school for girls from 1847 to 1850. In 1851, A. W. Putnam sold the property to Owen Frank, F. Regnier and George W. Barker. Frank resided there for many years and was credited with planting bald cypress trees, mistakenly called larch trees. After his death, the Washington County Board of Education used the house for classrooms. In 1918, the Crams family remodeled, named it the Larchmont, and opened it as a bed and breakfast. Over one hundred years after the house was built, Benjamin H. Putnam (also a descendent of Major Israel Putnam) bought the house and made extensive renovations. His granddaughter, Nancy, who later became the first woman mayor of Marietta, fondly remembered growing up there and claimed there was a spirit about the house that gave it a romantic charm. The house continued to be enjoyed by many new families and is a private residence today.

St. Luke's Episcopal Church
320 Second Street

A bishop of the Episcopal Diocese of Ohio visited Marietta in 1820, but at that time, there was no organized church because of the lack of clergy following the American Revolution. The Episcopal Church had to rely on missionaries to spread word to the frontier. The *Book of Common Prayer*, used in religious services of the Church of England and by local citizens, had come with the original pioneers to Marietta. In 1826, missionary Arius Nye founded the parish and services were held in homes. Judge Nye served as a lay reader for seven years. An 1833 church building was outgrown within twenty-five years and a new, larger building was built at the present site in 1856. Today, it is the oldest church building in Marietta still in use by its original denomination.

Today, the beautiful architecture of the church is hidden with large trees in front. The Gothic Revival style has a stately appearance with the four corner steeples, a peaked façade over the entrance, and the pointed, narrow windows. John M. Slocomb, the church's designer, was the premier Marietta architect of his day. Additions to the original design have been the library, organs, stained glass windows, pews, carpeting, offices, classrooms, and a memorial garden.

Washington County Courthouse
205 Putnam Street

Washington County, named after George Washington, was the first county created in what would become the state of Ohio. As the population of Washington County grew, the need for bigger and better courthouses followed. In 1797, the first courthouse was built on the corner opposite the present building. Citizens were aided in timekeeping when the bell in the cupola sounded three times each day. The small community also heard the bell upon the death of any local citizen. In 1800, the population of the entire county was only about 5,500 people. However, it doubled in size by 1820 and, after some disagreements on location, a new courthouse was built at the present site in 1823. Joseph Barker, a master builder, designed the structure and moved the bell to this second building. Formerly, the site had been a place of punishment equipped with pillory, stocks, and a whipping post.

By the turn of the century, the population of the county was 48,245. A grander courthouse, built in 1902, stands on the same corner as the old one. The architectural style is Second Renaissance Revival with distinct horizontal lines denoting each story of rough and finished white Bedford stone. The basement is above ground to prevent floodwaters from reaching the main offices and courts. The 158-foot tower showcases a bell and clock. In the 1920's, the tower housed the first radio transmitting-receiving station in the area.

New Riley Block
203 Second Street

Better known today as "The Galley," the New Riley Block has been around since 1899. At the turn of the century, large buildings were called "blocks." The area around the corner of Second and Butler Streets was not prime property; it was a swamp. Colonel John Riley took note of the nearby railway station, Union Depot, and built this three-story brick structure as a business venture. A furniture company occupied the first floor; the second floor was leased for a business and a labor organization; the third floor had rooms to rent.

It was not long before John M. Hackett, a successful oilman, recognized money could be made in the hotel business on the well-traversed corner. In 1902, Hackett's first floor saloon was famed as a place where a person could get a "free lunch" and enjoy a five-cent beer. Patrons could also relax with friends in the bowling alley, also located on the first floor. Upstairs, the Hackett Hotel often catered to people who had come to Marietta by train using Union Depot across the street. Hackett passed the business on to his son, Hanley, in 1965.

As future businesses would have it, the New Riley Block was destined to showcase Marietta's history. In 1981, the old Hackett Hotel was renovated and opened as the "Adventure Galley," a name associated with the flatboat used by Marietta's pioneers. The outstanding, original bar from the hotel and other memorabilia of days gone by was featured in the first floor restaurant. A banquet room was located on the second floor. In 2006, the building was updated and renamed "The Galley" with an outdoor patio. In 2010, "The Galley" opened the adjoining building as the Adelphia, a suggested early name for Marietta, which serves as a dance hall and concert theatre.

Tiber Way
1-12 Tiber Way

One of the most unusual architectural structures in Marietta is Tiber Way. In 1900, the curved building was hailed as a major downtown improvement. Colonel J. H. Riley, the owner, had the foresight to create business opportunity at a site that was deemed good for nothing. Originally, the swampy area was of a much lower elevation, with Goose Run forming a creek to the Muskingum River. A curved elevated rail line ran nearby, connecting Harmar with the Union Depot on Second Street. The building was designed to match the curve of the railroad track. To construct the new building, a nine-foot-in-diameter drain was laid for the creek and fill dirt added to be level with the railroad. The land improvement and building was a remedy for an unsightly nuisance that had also been a health menace. The building was named Tiber Way for the original name of Goose Run.

The building was divided into three sections with firewalls in between the partitions. The area fronting Second Street contained a two-story apartment where Colonel Riley maintained a residence for a number of years. The other two sections consisted of business space on the street level and a number of rooms and apartments on the two upper floors. The westernmost section, at one time, served as the Marietta Sanitarium, formerly at the corner of Front and Butler Streets. It included Turkish and Russian baths as well as massage treatment. The Tiber Way sanitarium was to specialize in the treatment of chronic diseases.

The building flourished with activity and then fell into disrepair. In 1986, Tiber Way under went a renovation. The second and third floors are apartments, with the first level being home to small retail businesses.

Levee House Café
127 Ohio Street

The three-story building housing part of the Levee House Café is the only remaining original Ohio riverfront structure in Marietta. Ohio Street, the earliest business district, was formerly lined with dry goods and other supply stores, warehouses, hotels, restaurants, and taverns. The Flatiron District, as the first block was known, was an inviting place for boat workers, newly arrived immigrants, and overnight travelers. In time, the transient and rougher elements of the riverfront, particularly the nightlife, became objectionable to the local residents. As the Victorian Era rules reinforced the New England ideals of the descendents of the original pioneers, shops on Ohio Street fell out of favor with locals and stores moved to Front Street.

The Federal style three-story brick structure at 127 Ohio Street was erected around 1826 for Dudley Woodbridge, Jr., a dry goods dealer. His father, Dudley, Sr., had been the first merchant of the Northwest Territory and his store was located on Muskingum Street (this street does not exist today, because the rivers are wider and deeper). Dudley, Jr. placed his store in the newer Flatiron business district of Marietta. In time, many businesses moved to Front Street and Woodbridge sold the building. Later, this Ohio Street building became the La Belle Hotel, known by some as a brothel.

In 1911, the one-story building with a Flemish bond brick pattern was opened as a saloon. At one time, the two buildings joined and became the Braddock Liquor Store. The word "whiskey" and other ads were written on the sides of the building, but are slowly fading away. During the 1970's, nearly all of the original brick buildings of the riverfront were removed. This last remaining structure has been the Levee House Café since 1983.

The Flatiron District
Triangular-shaped block bordered by Ohio and Greene Streets coming to a point at Front Street

If you asked someone in Marietta where the Flatiron District is, you would be met with a bewildered expression. No one living today would use the term that was once common knowledge. If you had been in Marietta in the early 1800's, you would have been eager to go to the Flatiron District. It was the center for shopping!

Pioneers going west by way of the Ohio River looked forward to their arrival in Marietta, as it was heralded as a place of respite and safe haven after the harrowing river journey from the East. With boats docked along the wharf, weary travelers would walk up to Ohio Street to find thriving businesses with an offering of culture in the frontier. In the very early days, Picketed Point, located at the confluence of the Ohio and Muskingum Rivers, held the first cabins and shops. One of the first and favorite places for people to rest was Buell and Munsell's Old Red House Hall, located at the foot of Front Street along the Ohio River. Opening in 1789, it was Marietta's first tavern, boarding house, and hotel. But as commerce developed, the stores of the Flatiron District were located a bit east of the old "Picketed Point". The merchants established an air of sophistication in the businesses that were frequented by local citizens and visitors alike. River traffic supplied a seemingly unlimited supply of boats brimming with goods to be sold in the stores, as well as travelers seeking a new life in the frontier. The success of these early businesses enabled Marietta to sustain an economic growth and thrive into a proper New England style town, as was the intention of the founding fathers.

The Flatiron District - the triangular-shaped square bounded by Ohio Street, Second Street, Greene Street, and coming to a point at Front Street - was beneficially located for travelers and merchants. As commerce flourished, additional stores and services continued east on Ohio and Greene Streets, as well as the streets intersecting them. The Flatiron District was the sole business district for local citizens, but it had not been intended that way. Front and Putnam Streets, later to be the business area, had developed as residential areas in the early years of Marietta. In the original design of the city, Washington Street, five-blocks north of the confluence, was designed with a large width to accommodate Marietta's business, but commerce never left the riverfront. For many local citizens, a shopping trip to the Flatiron District meant crossing a low swamp and stream that occupied the area that would later become Butler, Second, and Third Streets. The lure and convenience of the river trade kept the businesses alive along the banks of the Ohio River.

Probably the name most remembered about the Flatiron District was Woodbridge, a family of merchants originally located at the "Point." Dudley Woodbridge, a 1788 pioneer, had Marietta's first retail shop in a two-story frame building near Muskingum and Post Streets. Woodbridge and his son, Dudley, Jr., ordered goods from the East to be delivered by boat at the wharf. In 1814, Major John L. Lewis ordered a boiler cylinder from Pittsburgh that, upon arrival, was placed at the point where Ohio and Greene Streets converged. Lewis never claimed the equipment when it arrived. Dudley Woodbridge, Jr. refused to remove it and the boiler part remained a fixture of the district. Later, the area at Front and Greene Streets was referred to as Boiler Corner. The cylinder remained partially imbedded in the ground and a plaque was installed to commemorate the story. Dudley Woodbridge, Jr. continued the family business in a new three-story building on Ohio Street in 1826. Today, this brick structure at 127 Ohio Street is the only remaining riverfront structure from the heyday of the Flatiron District.

The Flatiron District grew and flourished with business in the early to mid-1800's. Dr. John B. Regnier operated the first drug store until 1818 when Dr. John Cotton set up his business. David Anderson, the first jeweler, specialized in clocks. On Ohio Street, basic needs were met with a grocery and meat market. P. W. Kuhn was the cigar manufacturer, the Grange Store had clothing, the Best Brothers had a boat shop, and Hinkel's had a restaurant. An ale and beer hall provided relaxation.

By the 1860's, storeowners of the Flatiron District offered a variety of goods and services that would entice and delight shoppers. J. B. Hovey & Company, wholesale and retail grocers, offered foreign fruits and nuts, wood ware, and willow ware. Cadwallader & Tappen owned the Gallery of Art featuring photographs. Shoemakers, dry goods dealers, bakeries, and saloons profited. During the steamboat days, hotels and taverns abounded near the waterfront. The U.S. Hotel, Globe Hotel, and the La Belle Hotel on Ohio Street accommodated new settlers awaiting property, businessmen, and workmen from the boats. The National House, at the corner of Greene and Second Streets, boasted of its location in the center of the business district and close to the wharf. Emma's House welcomed German settlers to the area. There were more than a dozen hotels in the Flatiron District. Many of the hotels operated for years, but a growing commerce area on Front Street challenged the retail stores.

With growth in population, the advent of the railroad, and local prosperity, many merchants favored Front Street and developed a new business district that was well underway by the 1860's. The grocers and dry goods dealers offered a greater variety of fancy and imported goods. Tobacco dealers, tailors, suppliers of home furnishings, hardware stores, booksellers, tin ware, and marble dealers welcomed consumers. Popularity of retail stores in the Flatiron District slowly faded as larger and more diverse businesses occupied Front Street and other streets away from the Ohio River. With many buildings abandoned and in poor repair, much of the once popular Flatiron District was rendered undesirable and its importance lost in history.

1840's Ohio Street.
Courtesy of Washington County Public Library, Local History and Genealogy

1860's Front Street.
Courtesy of Washington County Historical Society.

Shipbuilding Monument
Ohio Street near the gazebo

With the opening of the Northwest Territory in the 1780's, the Ohio River was used as a major highway leading to the West. Shipbuilders in Marietta took advantage of the location and began building sailing ships as early as 1800. The first vessel, the 110-ton brig *St. Clair,* built by Stephen Devol, took cargo of flour and pork to Havana, Cuba. From there it purchased sugar and traded in Philadelphia. Commodore Abraham Whipple, the famed Revolutionary War naval officer who was the first to fire a gun at the British in the open seas, captained the ship. After the trade in Philadelphia, he sold the ship and returned to Marietta.

Whipple's journey was considered successful enough to spur major shipbuilding in Marietta. Local businessmen applied for a "port of clearance" from the federal government that allowed Marietta to become an official port of the United States. Being a port so far inland was unusual. Not surprisingly, a Marietta ship was once questioned as legitimate when it sailed into Liverpool, England bound for Russia. More than twenty-five sailing vessels were built between 1800 and 1807. The building of large ships came to a halt when President Jefferson's Embargo Act of 1807 was passed, limiting overseas trade.

As time passed and the embargo lifted, Marietta boatyards began building steamboats. During the 1820's, James Whitney was a major builder, but the most well-known shipyard was that of William Knox and sons. He opened his yard in 1832 and launched over seventy-five steamboats. The last ocean-going vessel, the *John Farnurn,* was built in 1847.

Old St. Mary's Catholic School
132 South Fourth Street

As some of the first Irish and German Roman Catholic immigrants arrived in Marietta, they attempted to provide a parochial education, but it was difficult. The Catholic Church had been established in 1838 and, about 1856, the congregation began to raise money for a parochial school. Each member paid twenty-five cents per month. A school was held for a time in an old storeroom. In 1858, the basement of the church served as a school for several years. In 1895, Father Woesman made it a priority to establish a permanent parochial school. St. Mary's Catholic School was dedicated in 1896 with three classrooms. The new school was next door to the church on South Fourth Street. In 1898, a wing was added to the school to house five Dominican Sisters. The school population rose to more than two hundred students. Eventually, the school included dormitories and music rooms.

For all the planning, expense, and hard work in establishing a school, it was only used for about fifteen years. The church and school were located near enough to the river to suffer repeated flooding. In fact, it was claimed that the church was flooded twelve times in twenty-four years. A new church was built in the highlands of Fourth Street and the school relocated to the basement of the church in 1909. By that time, in addition to the elementary grades, the school was offering three years of high school. The church subsequently sold the property on South Fourth Street. After a long period of various uses and abandonment, the Romanesque style structure was completely restored in 1981. Today, the remodeled building is used for office space.

Unitarian Universalist Church
232 Third Street

Standing stately on the corner of Third and Putnam Streets in downtown Marietta, the Unitarian Universalist Church is revered as one of the finest examples of Gothic Revival architecture west of the Appalachians. John M. Slocomb, famed architect and master builder, designed the church which was dedicated in 1857. Handmade bricks used for the main structure came from the clay taken from Sacra Via Parkway, a protected site of the prehistoric Hopewell culture. The original wrought-iron fence was made in Harmar by the local foundry of Putnam, Poole and Company. The interior hand-carved curving stairway leading to the balcony was crafted by a former slave, who gained his freedom in the south because of his skill in woodworking. Sala Bosworth, a noted Marietta artist, painted the mural behind the pulpit. The design was based on a painting by the English artist, Sir Charles Eastlake. Both works are entitled "Christ Weeping Over Jerusalem." The importance of historical and architectural preservation is noted by the presence of the original interior woodwork, windowsills, cornices, and casings. The original pews still show nameplates of families of the 1800's. The 1884 flood destroyed the original pipe organ.

The prominent land speculator and philanthropist, Nahum Ward, was well known in Marietta. In his home, he entertained dignitaries, such as Marquis de Lafayette (1825) and John Quincy Adams (1843). But there was another side to Ward. He dreamed of organizing a Unitarian Society and building a church. He personally funded the project for $25,000 and then sold it to the congregation for the sum of one dollar. In 1869, the Unitarians joined with the local Universalist Society who had been gathering in Marietta since 1817. The church has hosted celebrated guest speakers such as Ralph Waldo Emerson, William Howard Taft, and Lucretia Mott.

Bosworth-Biszantz House
316 Third Street

Large brick and stone homes were built as a result of the wealth flowing into Marietta in the late 1800's. This house is among the earliest marking an economic revival at the end of the Civil War.

Martin Pomeroy Wells of the merchant firm, Bosworth and Wells, built the Federal style rear section of the house in 1868. He transferred it to his nephew and business associate, Daniel P. Bosworth, in 1870. The Bosworth family, who lived there for seventeen years, had two sons with notable careers. Hobart Bosworth worked on Broadway in New York, before having a successful career in California as a silent movie actor and then as a producer, director, and writer of over twenty films. Welles Bosworth was an architect who worked on the restoration of Versailles and made his home near Paris, France, at "Villa Marietta." He is remembered for donating the steps for Erwin Hall at Marietta College. Both brothers were given honorary degrees by Marietta College.

In 1897, oilman Frank B. Biszantz, who was also the proprietor of the St. James Hotel, acquired the house. He added front parlors and the distinctive Queen Anne style tower. The large two-sided porch and round second floor window are typical for this style. It has been know locally as the Biszantz house for 85 years, although the last occupant was a son-in-law who died in 1982. The Biszantz heirs sold the house to the City of Marietta, which later sold it to the Chamber of Commerce. Renovation of the house included removing the white paint on the exterior brick.

Third Street School Annex
346 Third Street

Early schools existed in various forms until 1849 when Marietta Schools were organized into a graded system. A year later, a high school began on Scammel Street between Fourth and Fifth Streets. The Board of Education purchased the land on Third Street in 1866. The large red brick building on the corner originally contained six classrooms with twenty-foot ceilings. There was a basement under most of the building with foundation stones that went down eight to ten feet. Early blackboards were made on sanded walls with many coats of black paint, then trimmed with a wide molding. Originally, a very high iron fence surrounded the whole schoolyard.

The attractive smaller building to the right (pictured here) was an annex built in 1870 to the school on the corner. The school buildings were used for grades one through seven. In the late 1890's, due to the booming economy and population increase, all schools in Marietta were operating at full student capacity. Putnam School, sometimes called the Third Street School, was closed about 1918. The Board of Education sold the buildings at auction in 1928.

INTERESTING NOTE:
Marietta maintained "separate, but equal" schools for whites and blacks until the "Colored School" was closed in 1883. The decision was controversial. Many whites stated they were willing to pay taxes for separate schools. Many blacks opposed the closure on the grounds that it took away the teacher of their color and their children would be outnumbered by race in the classrooms. In the end, the decision was upheld because the Board feared that they could not find a replacement for the black teacher who had resigned to take a job elsewhere.

Crown Of Life Evangelical Lutheran Church
300 Wooster Street

The Methodist circuit rider system brought German-speaking preachers to the frontier to search out isolated immigrants. German immigrants in Marietta welcomed these riders into their homes. As early as 1839, immigrants of German descent organized worship services which were held in private homes.

This brick building became home to the German Methodist Episcopal Church about 1878. The Italianate design is highlighted with round head windows and a roofline supported by double brackets. It originally had a projecting central entrance rising to form a steeple and bell tower 110 feet high. In 1906, a Sunday School addition was built. Because American public sentiment about Germans was controversial at the time of World War I, this church, as many others, wanted to show national support. The German language used in worship services was changed to English and the name of the congregation was changed to Trinity Methodist Episcopal Church.

In 1969, the Christ United Methodist Church utilized the building until it was sold to the Crown of Life Evangelical Lutheran Church in 1986. The congregation completed extensive renovations. The Midmer reed organ, the only one in Marietta, with its unique lower pitch tones has been in continuous use since 1919, although a German master builder rebuilt it in 1987. Otto Brothers, successful German merchants in Marietta, had donated the pipe organ. The steeple, damaged in 1939 by lightning, was rebuilt at a reduced height and a cross was added.

Dawes House
508 Fourth Street

For almost seventy-five years, this house was the homestead of the Dawes family. Built in 1869 for Annette and Asa Waters, it was purchased the following year by Rufus R. and Mary B. Dawes. A decorated Civil War officer, Rufus Dawes led a regiment known as the Iron Brigade for which he was promoted to brevet brigadier general in 1865. After the war, he had a successful lumber business selling wholesale to the railroads. Because of his superior oration skills, Dawes was elected to Congress. From 1871-1899, he served on the Board of Trustees for Marietta College

His eldest son, Charles Gates Dawes, a Marietta College graduate, pursued two careers, one in business and finance, and the second in politics. Dawes is most known for being vice-president of the United States under Calvin Coolidge from 1925-1929. It is said that he received word of his nomination on the porch of this house. Dawes was honored with the Nobel Peace Prize in 1925 for his report on German reparations. The final post in his political career was that of U.S. Ambassador to the United Kingdom. In later years, Dawes returned to his earlier interests in banking and became chairman of the board of the City National Bank and Trust Co. in Evanston, Illinois.

The home has had several owners since the Dawes family. For almost twenty years it served as a convent for St. Mary's Catholic Church. Today, it is a private residence.

Basilica of St. Mary of the Assumption
500 Fourth Street

The first Roman Catholic services were held in Marietta on South Fourth Street in the late 1830's. The early church building had stained glass windows, a spire, and a set of three bells. The flood of 1884 rose over the altar, and the subsequent floods of 1891, 1895, and 1898 were calls to the small congregation to move out of the flood plain to higher ground.

In 1900, plans were made to purchase the corner of Fourth and Wooster Streets, a site out of the flood plain and looking over the city. This corner lot was occupied by a large house which had, for a time, been the Elizabeth College for Women. The building was moved to the adjoining lot to the north. This building's architectural design complemented the grandeur of the church and became the parish rectory. It took four weeks to move the house to its new foundation.

As visitors approach the Roman Catholic Church, the largest church in Marietta, they are awed by the size and design, especially the towers and dome that highlight Marietta's landscape. The architect described it as a "Spanish Renaissance" style, with a blend of Romanesque and Gothic. Construction began in 1903 and was completed in 1909 with the structure rising in excess of one hundred feet in height from its base on Fourth Street. The grandness of the interior of the church is emphasized by huge pillars supporting the spectacular nave lit by the huge round stained glass window in the front and small stained glass windows on the sides. Large round stained glass windows are also at each end of the transept. These windows were made in Munich, Germany, and brought through the British blockade during World War I. The wall of the apse holds a sculpture of the Virgin Mary surrounded by cherubs. The church was renovated in the 1970's and most recently in 2008. In 2013, St. Mary Church was designated a Minor Basilica by Pope Francis.

Shipman-Mills House
430 Fourth Street

Sitting on a corner lot high above the sidewalk, the painted brick Victorian Gothic style home is entertained by the sound of bells of nearby churches. The ornate decorative bargeboards on the gables added with stylish slender posts and brackets supporting the porches give the house a commanding presence. Built in 1852 by John B. Shipman, it was probably one of the first of the neighborhood.

After several owners, the Mills family purchased it in 1877. In 1865, John Lawrence Mills, a Yale graduate, joined the faculty of Marietta College as a professor of math and Latin. His wife, Elizabeth, also was interested in education and had taught English, French, and music. With their combined intellectual backgrounds, the Mills had the foresight to create a special institution of higher learning.

In 1890, Professor Mills established Elizabeth College, providing an institution of higher learning for women. The school conducted classes in the corner house across Wooster Street from the Mills's home. A local newspaper at the time stated that women deserved an education and the school should be supported. In 1894, Marietta College took over control and renamed it the Marietta College for Women until the campus became coeducational in 1897. The school building was bought by the Roman Catholic Church and moved to 502 Fourth Street about 1900. The old school became the home for the priest who served the church.

The Castle
418 Fourth Street

The Castle is one of the best examples of Gothic Revival style architecture in Ohio. Special attractions of the house are the octagonal tower, a trefoil attic window, and stone-capped spires. The front of the property is lined by a cut stone wall and a Victorian cast iron fence revealing a brick and stone sidewalk on an elevated terrace. The interior features a scagliola fireplace mantle, coodge papier-mache mouldings, and floor to ceiling, self-storing shutters on the front bay window. John M. Slocomb designed the Castle.

Several prominent citizens have called the Castle home. Melvin Clarke, a local attorney and abolitionist, began construction in 1855 until he sold the property in 1858. Later, he lost his life in the Civil War. John Newton, agent for the Marietta Bucket Factory, purchased the home. He and his family enjoyed entertaining in the home for over twenty-five years. Edward W. Nye, publisher of *The Marietta Gazette*, purchased the estate in 1887, but only lived here a year before his death. The house was passed on to his daughter, Lucy Nye Davis, who was married to Theodore Davis, state senator and president pro tem. Her eldest daughter and heir, Jessie, was fourteen when her mother inherited the home. Jessie lived in the Castle until her death five days before her one-hundredth birthday in 1974. Because she never wanted to leave this house, her funeral was held there.

The Castle was renovated by Stewart Bosley and his sister, Bertlyn, and deeded to the Betsey Mills Corporation in 1992, "as an historical asset for the City of Marietta with such asset to be used for educational and public purposes." Educational programs, tours, and special events are held throughout the year.

St. Luke's Lutheran Church
401 Scammel Street

By the 1830's, the German Lutheran population in Marietta met together in their homes for worship. In 1837 and 1838, Reverend C. L. F. Haensel, an Episcopal rector from Germany, occasionally provided services and sacraments. In 1839, the German Evangelical Church (now St. Paul's Evangelical) was founded. They worshipped together, but the Lutherans withdrew in 1857. The Lutherans organized the German Evangelical St. Lukas Church in 1858 in the former St. Luke's Episcopal Church at Fourth and Scammel Streets, adopting the same saint's name, the German St. Lukas. The Reverend K. F. Thieme, pastor in the 1890's replaced German language services with English, which resulted in increased membership.

In 1901, a new green fieldstone Neo-Romanesque church was erected on the same lot. When walking into the church, one's eyes are immediately drawn to the exquisite woodcarving of the Lord's Supper, a replica of the painting by Leonardo da Vinci. Alois Lang, master woodcarver born in Oberammergau, Germany, was from the famed Lang family of the Passion Play. In 1988, there was an extensive fire in the church, but the priceless woodcarving survived, needing only to be cleaned of soot. In 1992, a two-story addition on the north side of the church was completed using matching stone to the original to give the appearance of one continuous structure; a small chapel was also added. Today, the bright red door of the church is a distinguishing and inviting feature.

Betsey Mills Club
300 Fourth Street

In 1898, Betsey Gates Mills started a Sewing Club for girls from the Pike Street area. The Girls' Monday Club, as it came to be called by 1911, needed a home. William and Betsey Mills purchased the Beman Gates home on the corner of Fourth and Putnam, where Betsey had been born as well as her famous nephew, Charles Gates Dawes. The Girls' Monday Club provided not only sewing lessons, but also life skills for the girls who did not have the opportunity to go to college.

After Betsey's death in 1920, William Mills announced plans to honor his wife with the construction of a building complex consisting of a dining room, a gymnasium, and a clubhouse. In 1924, the Monday Club changed its name to the Betsey Mills Club. Mr. Mills also bought the Edgar W. Hopp property on the northern adjoining lot. Both houses were remodeled and joined under one roof. A gymnasium and swimming pool were added in 1926. The new complex was dedicated in 1927 "to serve the girls and women in Marietta and vicinity in such a way as to promote Christian character and service…" In time, the facility broadened its services. Interestingly, in the late 1920's, Marietta College used the Betsey Mills club to fulfill required physical education classes for women. Today, the Betsey Mills Club is a lasting icon of Marietta, originally donated to serve women, but later providing a space for the entire community to hold meetings and receptions, conduct classes, and dine.

The Betsey Mills Club is a Georgian red brick structure with Flemish bond. Stone arches above the doors and stone lintels over windows are highlights in the symmetry of this building. Twenty-two-inch thick walls support the structure. The very durable copper roof over the entire building has stood the test of time, as have the steel trusses under the roof.

Macmillen House
213 Fourth Street

The McMillen family was an early occupant of this nineteenth century home, now a part of the Marietta College campus. At one time, Samuel McMillen was editor of *The Marietta Times*, a Democratic newspaper. Francis McMillen was born in 1885 and became a child prodigy who achieved an international reputation as a fine violinist. At age ten, he performed in a Chicago concert that led to eleven years of study in Europe. In 1902, when McMillen was sixteen, he won first prize at the annual contest of the Brussels Royal Conservatory of Music. His American debut at Carnegie Hall in New York City in 1907 brought him back to the U.S., where he toured extensively. At some point during his rising fame, he changed the spelling of his last name to Macmillen. At the age of twenty-two, he was internationally famous and lived in Europe for over twenty years. In 1926, Macmillen gave a concert in Marietta and remarked, "…Marietta is an exceptional place… this city has much more evidence of culture and refinement than is apparent in other cities its size." In 1935, he received an honorary degree from Marietta College. The DAR marked his birthplace as a historic site in 1938.

The thirteen-room painted brick house was built in 1846-1847 by Silas Slocomb. As common with the style, a rectangular transom with sidelights frames the doorway. The façade of Flemish bond, the two immured chimneys, and original louvered shutters are distinctive features. Today, the structure is owned by Marietta College which has adapted the building for use as the physical plant.

Marietta College Campus
Intersection of Fifth and Putnam Streets

Marietta College is one of the oldest, continually operating colleges in Ohio. Its roots come from the 1797 Muskingum Academy, the first institution of higher learning in the Northwest Territory. Rufus Putnam and other early pioneers determined to make education an important asset of their town as a way to secure New England refinement and culture. The Institute of Education and the Marietta Collegiate Institute and Western Teachers' Seminary of the 1830's played a part in paving the way for a college. Marietta College, a small, private, liberal arts college, was chartered in 1835 with a degree program taught by only five professors. In 1876, Charles Sumner Harrison of Marietta was heralded as the first black alumnus. With education for women being controversial in the 1890's, Marietta College broke the gender barrier by having the first co-ed graduation class in 1898.

Marietta College offers a beautiful campus rich in history, diversity, and excellence. Occupying nearly 100 acres, Marietta College offers a beautiful campus rich in history, diversity, and excellence. Students from around the United States and over ten nations walk the campus and the streets of Marietta. Many notable people, such as Betty Friedan, Ralph Nader, Martin Luther King, Jr., Doris Kearns Goodwin, David Brinkley, and United States presidents, have visited Marietta College to enhance not only collegiate life, but also to enrich the lives of the community. Preservation of historic buildings on the campus gives honor to the past importance of higher education in the pioneer city. Marietta College is listed as one of America's thirty-seven "Revolutionary Colleges" with origins in the eighteenth century.

Mills Home
301 Fifth Street

The Mills home is better known as the Marietta College President's Home. This classical structure overlooking the campus of Marietta College has watched the school grow from a couple of buildings into a respected Midwest college. Professors, students, prominent citizens, and many influential guests have visited the home over the years. In 1910, when it was the home of the Mills family, President William H. Taft was an honored guest for the Seventy-Fifth Anniversary of Marietta College.

Henry P. Wilcox, Marietta's eighth postmaster, purchased the property in 1821, removed a framed house and built a two-story brick Federal style house in 1822. Great attention was given to the construction of the home to secure it on this hilltop perch. Timbers were hand-hewn, mortised and tenoned together, and often secured by wooden pins. The basement walls were made twenty-four inches thick. Wilcox, however, mysteriously disappeared on New Year's Day in 1825. Local legend suggests that Wilcox pilfered funds from the post office and, once exposed, left town, making Governor Return Jonathon Meigs, Jr. (a long time friend) responsible for the home.

Colonel John Mills, Sr., prominent businessman, banker, and treasurer of Marietta College, acquired the house in the mid- 1830's. Mills's business affairs enabled Marietta to prosper by his interests in several banks, the Marietta Chair Company, the Marietta Gas Company, and the Marietta and Cincinnati Railroad. He took great pride in the house and entertained local and national celebrities. Mills enlarged the house, giving it a Greek Revival style entrance, and improved the grounds. He added side porches and the front portico. The portico entrance boasts a flat-arched stone lintel with elliptical fanlight and sidelights. The stone wall and curved iron railing near the front entrance give the house an imposing presence. Colonel Mills died in 1882 and left the house to his sons, John, Jr. and W. W. Mills, both Marietta College graduates and trustees of the college. The home and carriage house were purchased by Marietta College in 1937. It has been the home of Marietta College presidents since that time.

Marietta College - Erwin Hall
Christy Mall

Erwin Hall, the oldest academic building on the campus, has been a long-time symbol for Marietta College. The cornerstone was laid at the commencement ceremonies in 1845. The three-story Greek Revival design was distinguished by the twelve immured chimneys along the eaves and the square clock tower with bell. With construction completed by 1850, the sounding of the bell was heard daily in the downtown area as a reminder that Marietta could boast that an institution of higher learning was in session.

The Marietta and Harmar communities played an instrumental role in the creation of this building. With a donation by William Slocomb, interest in the project was intensified, but more funds had to be raised for the $10,000 structure. Subscriptions to support construction ranged from $1.00 to $200.00. The subscriptions took the form of goods, building materials, and labor, as well as money. For example: a Washington County farmer quarried, dressed, and hauled the stone for the sills and original steps. The subscription book contains nearly two hundred names of contributors. As additional aid for construction came from other parts of the county, Marietta College proudly claimed two buildings for its campus.

This iconic structure has a history of changing names and purposes. In the 1850's, it was used as a library with lecture halls, space for literary societies, and a chapel. Later, it was referred to as the middle building and, then, the science building. In 1894, it was named after Cornelius B. Erwin, a generous benefactor of the college. New steps, installed in 1924, were the gift of Dr. Welles Bosworth, a Marietta native who became a notable architect in the United States and France. Major interior renovations took place in the 1970's. Presently, it houses the Education program.

Marietta College - Andrews Hall
Christy Mall

Andrews Hall, one of the oldest buildings on the Marietta College campus, was named after Israel Ward Andrews, a mathematician, political scientist, and a president of the college. Upon his death in 1888, he bequeathed half of his estate to the college. Much of the funds for construction came from alumni who wanted to honor the memory of Andrews. The character of the Romanesque style building offered a quality of strength with its massive form, thick walls, arched doorway, and tower. The cornerstone was laid in 1891.

Originally, Andrews Hall was designed to house Marietta Academy, the College's preparatory Department. Through the years, Andrews has served as both classroom and office building. It has held the college president's office, a chapel, and a theater. In the 1980's, the building was in danger of demolition, but because of concern of alumni, faculty, and friends of the college, the decision was reversed and the interior of the historic building was completely reconstructed and refurbished to serve as a student center. It was reopened in 1993. Andrews Hall serves the needs of students, staff and greater campus life, especially with the great room that is capable of handling performances, special exhibits, and large group activities. The spacious, light room showcases the building's original stained glass windows. The building serves as space for student organization activities, with a snack bar, meeting rooms, and lounges.

Flanders House
505 Putnam Street

From the wall of cut stone at the sidewalk to the cupola on the roofline, this house has watched over the growing campus of Marietta College. In 1848, the house was built in a Federal style, but after a fire, it was remodeled as an Italianate style. The decorative cupola with observation rail, sometimes called a "Widow's Walk," was typical of the Italianate style of nineteenth century architecture in New England. In myth, the wife of a seafarer would stand on this perch to await his return. As ships sailed from the Port of Marietta, the "Widow's Walk" was an appropriate feature.

Several prominent families have occupied this home. Thomas W. Ewart, the first owner, was one of the youngest members elected to represent Washington and Morgan Counties at the Constitutional Convention of 1850 that formed the present-day constitution for the state of Ohio. Theodore D. Dale, founder of the Marietta Electric Company, and his descendents lived in the house for many years. Most significantly, Mr. Dale was credited for the construction of railroads that linked Marietta with the north and the west. In 1889, Dale initiated the plan to have all railroad lines coming into Marietta end at one terminus. The low, swampy land on Second Street was filled with dirt and Union Station was built. For a brief time, Dr. W. R. Dabney occupied the home. In 1912, J. Edwin Flanders bought the home. Edward J. Flanders of Flander Brothers' Insurance and his descendents resided here for about sixty years.

George White House
322 Fifth Street

William P. Skinner, a successful early merchant and the second sheriff, built this house in 1855 and lived here until his death in 1866. In 1908, Charlotte McKelvey White, wife of George White, purchased the house. George White, born in New York and raised in Pennsylvania, was no stranger to the oil business in which he would make his fortune. He was a teenager in Titusville, birthplace of the modern oil industry, when this city was at its peak of oil production. White attended Princeton University, briefly taught school, and in 1898 participated in the Klondike gold rush. He made money and invested in the oil industry, eventually owning wells in many states including Ohio.

In 1902, White settled in Marietta and began his political career, first as a Democrat in the Ohio Legislature and then in the U.S. House of Representatives. In 1920, he became the Chairman of the Democratic National Committee. White was also a Marietta College Board trustee and vice-president of People's Banking and Trust Company. During the Great Depression years, White served two-year terms as governor and created the Ohio Highway Patrol. George White was the third person from Marietta to be Governor of Ohio.

The house is of Greek Revival style with its symmetrical design and row of dentils encircling the house under the eaves. The third floor was added to accommodate the growing White family. The Alpha Xi Delta Sorority bought the house in 1954 and made many changes to the interior.

House Of Seven Porches
331 Fifth Street

Marietta College mathematics professor Diarca Howe Allen, a New Hampshire native, built this unique home in 1835 when he moved here from Charleston, South Carolina. D. H. Allen was one of the five original professors to teach at Marietta College when it was chartered in 1835. This area of Fifth Street was once referred to as "Professor's Row" and Allen's home was one of the first.

D. H. Allen wanted his home to have the appeal of his New England and Charleston, South Carolina experiences. The two-story porches supported by Doric columns on the north and south sides of the house give a southern flavor to this Greek Revival style. The three tiers of porches in the rear of the home continue this southern influence.

The interior design of the house continues a combination of New England and southern style. Painted woodwork, six over six windows, six panel doors, and unadorned banisters and balusters on the staircases are typical for early colonial homes. In the front parlor, jib doors with double hung windows above them open to allow free access to the front porches, similar to what you would see in the South. Originally, the kitchen and dining room were located on the lowest level to keep the heat out of the upper rooms during the summer.

Following the residency of D.H. Allen, several different owners enjoyed the house. John Oliver Cram purchased the home in 1840 and built a carriage house with living quarters. It became known as "The Buell House" because of the lengthy occupancy by members of this family. Members of the J. Herbert Otto family called the house home for fifty years, during which Jean Kelso, daughter-in-law, opened it as a bed and breakfast for a time. Presently, it is a private residence.

St. Paul's Evangelical Church
401 Fifth Street

A significant number of German-speaking people were migrating to Marietta in the early nineteenth century. In 1838, a German religious society was formed which served all Protestant groups of Christian German-speaking immigrants. After some differences, a group established the German United Evangelical Church in 1840 and began raising money for a single-room building at the corner of Fifth and Scammel Streets. The first Sunday School began in 1848. John Slocomb, the architect, completed the structure in 1849 and the congregation continued to grow. More room was needed, so in 1872 the vestibule and balcony were added and the name was changed to St. Paul's Evangelical Church. After seventy years and twenty-two German-speaking ministers, the language of the service was changed to English in 1909.

In 1932, the growing membership made some changes. Memorial art glass windows were installed and a brick addition was constructed at the rear for an organ chamber, choir room, and pastor's study. In 1934, the Evangelical Church merged with the Reformed Church and the local church became St. Paul's Evangelical and Reformed Church. Later, this denomination combined with the Congregational Church to become the United Church of Christ. In 2004, the name was restored to St. Paul's Evangelical Church to reaffirm the Evangelical faith. Today, to memorialize the German heritage of Marietta, the German word "kirche," meaning church, is still written above the door of St. Paul's Evangelical Church.

Mound Cemetery
Fifth Street at intersection of Scammel Street

Mound Cemetery square was set aside by early pioneers as a public space to protect part of the extensive earthworks in Marietta. The prehistoric ceremonial burial mound, named Conus by the pioneers, is 30 feet high and 115 feet wide at its base. Mostly, the remaining earthworks in Marietta are attributed to the Hopewell culture, but many believe the Mound to be the work of the Adenas, an earlier prehistoric people. You can enjoy the view atop the mound by climbing a flight of forty-six hand-carved stone steps and sitting on a park bench.

Mound Cemetery is said to be the burial place of more Revolutionary War officers than any other single cemetery in the United States. Many war veterans were encouraged by the government to seek lands in the Northwest Territory as a partial payment for service and to bring law and order to the frontier. They came and they stayed. Mound Cemetery came into existence about 1801 when Col. Robert Taylor, Revolutionary War veteran of Rhode Island, was interred. He was the first of more than twenty-five veterans, including Brigadier General Rufus Putnam, leader of the 48 Pioneers of 1788, to be buried there. Burial sites of these men appear on the colorful Washington County Historical Society marker placed near the moat around the mound.

The Mound Square is named for Marie Antoinette, in honor of the French queen for which Marietta is named. Rufus Putnam, to whom the land had been leased in 1789, gave Square No. 1 to the city of Marietta. When a shallow excavation of the mound was done and skeletal remains were found, the mound was determined to be an ancient burial site and no further excavations occurred. An action by the trustees in 1811 allowed the entire Mound Square to be used as the town cemetery. The area of Mound Cemetery and Conus Mound was the first historic site protected by an act of law in the United States.

Josiah D. Cotton House
412 Fifth Street

As you travel on Fifth Street, the Cotton House stands out as something special. This two-story Greek Revival brick house was built in 1853. The gallery porches on each side of the house give it a palatial southern feel. The temple front façade, topped by a pediment with a fan shaped window, and the recessed doorway give the house an imposing look. Outstanding dentils are repeated in the pediment under the gable.

Josiah D. Cotton, a graduate of Marietta College in 1842, studied medicine with his father, a practicing physician in Marietta. Cotton also studied in New Orleans and in Ohio before receiving his degree at the University of Louisville, Kentucky. When his father died in 1847, he assumed the medical practice in Marietta. Cotton served for three years in the Civil War as a surgeon of the Ninety-Second Ohio Volunteer Infantry. He was one of the oldest members of the Ohio State Medical Society and a member of the American Medical Association. Cotton was active in local politics as a member of Marietta Council for ten years. He died in 1903.

Willia, Cotton's daughter, graduated in the first coed graduation class from Marietta College. She was a librarian for many years and lived in the house long after her parents were gone. Since 1919, the home has had several owners.

Clark-Van Metre House
515 Fifth Street

John Clark, a native of Quincy, Massachusetts, came to Marietta about 1794. Here he was a major in the militia and the Sheriff of Washington County (1803-1810). The rear section of the house was built in 1800 and later additions included front parlors and columns. For some reason, the deed was not recorded until 1851, a few months before his death at age eighty-four. Clark willed the house to his wife, Loranna, for her lifetime and then to three daughters. Great-granddaughter Grace Applegate married Wyllis Van Metre in 1895. Both had graduated from college and were born into successful families. Van Metre operated the S.R. Van Metre Company, a popular clothing store on Front Street, with his father. S. R. Van Metre opened the first clothing store in 1877, and also had interest in several insurance companies in his later years. Grace and Wyllis lived with his parents at 427 Fourth Street before acquiring the home on Fifth Street in the early 1900's. Grace lived there until her death at the age of 101 in 1972.

Many homes in the early 1800's were of Federal style, but this house has a Greek Revival style look due to later additions. Symmetrical placement of the windows gives it a Federal look. The upper right shutters conceal what appears to be a window. Actually, there is no window in this area of the house, but the symmetry is maintained. The two-story portico was added later with fluted columns topped by Doric capitals to give it a grand Greek Revival entrance. A second floor door to a small porch adds to the overall look of the front exterior of the home.

Major Clark's son built a similar house at the nearby corner of Fifth and Wooster Streets for his sister. It is also Greek Revival style and is an imposing presence on the corner.

Thomas Cisler House
340 Seventh Street

This Queen Anne/Eastlake style house is difficult to see in the summer because it is surrounded in trees. Thomas Cisler's brick house was built in 1885 on a ridge that originally overlooked the family brick-making business, which was located where the YMCA is today. Great attention was given to architectural details so that no two facades are alike. Fish scale shingles at some of the gabled ends and zinc lintels over the windows are some of the distinguishing features. The fan motif in the pediment is striking as you approach the front entrance.

Thomas H. Cisler, a Marietta College graduate, usually gets the credit for the house and the business, but it was Thomas, his father who built the house and inherited the brickyard from his father, Heinrich, a native of Germany. Thomas Cisler & Son, brick manufacturers, were responsible for many brick buildings in Marietta and for the nearly six miles of brick streets. The brickyards are gone, but the nearby brick houses still standing on Seventh Street were the workmen's houses and grocery. When the brick plant closed, Cisler donated land for the YMCA, Ephraim Cutler Street, a Marietta College observatory, and other property to the college.

Cisler, a prominent business leader, also was a civic leader fostering religious and cultural interests within the community. He played the organ for his church for 26 years, organized Marietta Astronomical Society and the Marietta Bach Society that met in the Cisler home. Lillian, his daughter, continued the society following his death in 1950. Lillian was an expert in the history of Marietta, a theologian, and expert of world missions.

Old Children's Home
360 Muskingum Drive

Catherine Fay Ewing, credited with initiating the Children's Home System in Ohio, came to Marietta in 1833 with her father. Catherine attended Marietta Female Seminary, became a teacher, and took a job in Oklahoma working with Choctaw Indian children. During her ten-year stay, Catherine experienced the plight of children who were abused or left homeless by family tragedies.

In 1857, Catherine returned to Ohio and bought 12 acres of land near Moss Run in Washington County. Nine very young orphans were soon under her care. During the Civil War, she found orphaned children housed at the county infirmary. Catherine petitioned the government to take responsibility for the "war" orphans. Through the efforts of State Senator Samuel Knowles of Marietta, a law was passed in 1866 that allowed for tax-supported children's homes.

Washington County purchased a one hundred acre farm on Muskingum Drive. On April 11, 1867, Catherine Fay Ewing moved 35 children from her home to the new state-supported Children's Home. Washington County Children's Home was the first tax-supported children's home in the nation. Because of Ewing, the plan originating in Ohio became the model for states across the nation.

The home operated for many years, caring for hundreds of children. In the 1970's, the state closed the children's homes and replaced them with the foster parent program. Today, the buildings are used for child, health, and welfare services. Nearby, on land that was part of the original complex, is Ewing School named in honor of Catherine Fay Ewing.

Afterward

As you have traversed the streets of Marietta, many homes, unmentioned in this writing, have probably been of interest for their architecture and hidden history. It was not unusual for builders to fashion a bit of Victorian fancy upon a home or to place a turret or tower to form a more interesting aspect to even a fairly simple structure. The first owners of these homes were part of the building blocks forming the culture and charm of Marietta today.

If you have taken the entire tour presented in this book, then you have invested a lot of time. It is my hope that the information and photographs have given you a richer sense of why people seem to be drawn into the ambiance of this Ohio River city. The building of this New England style town, as first envisioned by the early pioneers, developed in stages as businesses nestled close to the rivers, then moved uptown. As the United States expanded to the West, railroads and highways linked Marietta to other communities by land. The once busy Port of Marietta now serves as a venue for entertainment, rather than a place of river commerce. Historic homes, buildings and monuments of Marietta remain as an inheritance, living mementos to utilize, preserve, and share.

Glossary Of Architectural Terms

Bargeboards – Decorative boards fitted at the edge of gables.

Bracket – Often associated with the Italianate Style of the mid-nineteenth century. Support boards, which may be structural or decorative, projecting under eaves, windows, or cornices.

Corbel – A singular projecting stone or a series of stones as in an arch that supports weight above it.

Cornice – Horizontal molding projecting along the top of a building, wall, or arch.

Dentil – A small square block used in a series for decoration, especially under a cornice.

Fanlight – A semicircular window with radiating panes of glass, usually over a door or window.

Federal style architecture – Features may include the following: a low pitched roof, windows arranged symmetrically with a central doorway, semicircular fanlight over the front door, narrow side windows on each side of the front door, decorative roof over front door, dentil molding in the cornice, Palladian windows, circular or elliptical windows, and shutters. This style was popular from 1780 to 1840.

Georgian style architecture – Features may include the following: a square, symmetrical shape, front door at the center, decorative crown over the front door, flattened columns on each side of door, five windows across front, paired chimneys, median pitched roof, and minimal roof overhang. This style was popular from the 1690's to 1830.

Gothic Revival style architecture – Features may include the following: a steep-pitched roof, steep gables, windows with pointed arches, vertical board-and-batten siding, and a one-story porch. This style was popular from 1840 to 1880.

Greek Revival style architecture – Features may include the following: a wide, pedimented gable; symmetrical shape; heavy cornice; wide, plain frieze; and simple moldings. Sometimes structures have an entry portico with tall columns and sidelight windows around the front door. The style was popular from 1825 to 1860.

Italianate style architecture – Features may include the following: a low-pitched or flat roof; symmetrical rectangular shape; tall appearance, with two, three, or four stories; wide overhanging eaves with brackets and cornices; square cupola; porch topped with balconies; tall, narrow, double-paned windows; side bay windows; and heavily molded doors. This style was popular from 1840 to 1885.

Lintel – A horizontal stone or board support between two columns, posts, or the opening of a window or door.

Pediment – The triangular space forming the gable of buildings or over porticos. It may be found above doors and windows.

Pilaster – A flat, slightly projected column, attached to a wall.

Queen Anne style architecture – Features may include the following: steep roof; complex irregular shape; front facing gables; one-story porch that extends across one or two sides of the house; round or square towers; decorative shingles on walls; patterned masonry; ornamental spindles or brackets, and bay windows. This style was popular from 1880 to 1890.

Romanesque style architecture – Features may include the following: massive quality, thick walls, rounded arches around windows and doors, and towers.

Transom – A horizontal stone or wood support that separates a door from a window above.

Victorian style architecture – Victorian architecture was not really a style, but refers to a period of time in history in which lacy and ornamental details were added to structures. It was popular from 1840 to 1900.

Widow's Walk – A small observation platform often with a decorative railing, frequently found on the roofs of eighteenth and nineteenth century houses in New England and the Atlantic seaboard.

Selective Bibliography

Andrews, Martin. *History of Marietta and Washington County, Ohio And Representative Citizens.* Chicago, IL: Biographical Publishing Company, 1902.

Austin, L. G. General Compiler. *Illustrated Historical and Business Review of Washington County, Ohio For the Year 1891.* Coshocton, OH: 1891.

Beach, Arthur G. *Pioneer College, The Story of Marietta,* Privately Printed: 1935.

Cayton, Andrew R. L., Paula Riggs, and Robert Frank Cayton, Ed. *City Into Town: The City of Marietta, Ohio, 1788-1988.* Marietta, OH: Marietta College Dawes Memorial Library, 1991.

Cottle, Elizabeth Stanton Ed. *The American Association of University Women, A Window To Marietta, 2 nd Ed. Marietta OH:* Richardson Printing Company, 1996.

Gerke, Robert H. "Marietta In the Gay Nineties." The Marietta Times Apr. 1970. (Reprinted from 1939)

Hawley, Owen P. "Pioneers Got Down To Business." *Marietta Ohio 1796-1996.* Marietta, OH: Marietta Bicentennial Commission, 1996.

History of Washington County, Ohio, 1788-1881. Cleveland, OH: H. Z. Williams & Brother Publishing, 1881.

Howe, Jeffery, Ed. *The Houses We Live In.* London: PRC Publishing Limited, 2003.

Lindley, Harlow, Chairman. *The Ordinance of 1787 and the Old Northwest Territory.* USA, 1937.

Marietta Board of Trade. *Century Review of Marietta, Ohio.* Marietta OH: 1900. (Reprinted by the Washington County Historical Society), 2006.

Marietta City and Washington County Directory of 1898. Marietta, OH: W. H. Armitage, Publisher, 1898.

Marietta City Directory 1900. Marietta, OH: W. H. Armitage Publisher, 1900.

Sheppard's Marietta City Directory for 1873 and 1874. Cincinnati, OH: J. S. Sheppard & Company, Publisher, 1874.

Summers, Thomas J. *History of Marietta.* Marietta, OH: The Leader Publishing Company, 1903.

William's Marietta Directory, City Guide and Business Mirror for 1860 and 1861. Marietta, OH: C. E. Glines Publisher, 1861.

Numerous sources were cited from the following: the subject files, name files, and family histories found at the Washington County Public Library's Local History and Genealogy Department, and *The Tallow Light* published by Washington County Historical Society.

About the Author

Local Marietta history has always held a special interest for Jann K. Adams. As a child, she was aware of the family's German heritage. Her immigrant great-grandfather operated the Marietta Brewing Company at the turn of the twentieth century. Growing up in Marietta, Jann enjoyed the brick streets, Victorian buildings, and the prehistoric mounds as a childhood playground.

Jann taught social studies for Marietta City Schools before pursuing her research in local German and Marietta history. She has been a guide for Trolley Tours. Inc. in Marietta, has presented programs on the influence of Germans in Marietta, and has been a guide for Ghost Trek, a tour of historic hauntings in Marietta. Jann is a member of the Washington County Historical Society.